A HOLE in the WALL

I Like to Read® books, created by award-winning
picture book artists as well as talented newcomers,
instill confidence and the joy of reading in new readers.

We want to hear every new reader say, "I like to read!"

Visit our website for flash cards, activities, and more about the series:
www.holidayhouse.com/ILiketoRead
#ILTR
This book has been tested by an educational expert
and determined to be a guided reading level D.

I LIKE TO READ is a registered trademark of Holiday House Publishing, Inc.
Copyright © 2016 by Hans Wilhelm
All Rights Reserved
HOLIDAY HOUSE is registered in the U.S. Patent and Trademark Office.
Printed and bound in September 2022 at Toppan Leefung, DongGuan City, China.
The artwork was created with digital tools and pencil.
www.holidayhouse.com
3 5 7 9 10 8 6 4

Library of Congress Cataloging-in-Publication Data
Wilhelm, Hans, 1945– author, illustrator.
A hole in the wall / Hans Wilhelm. — First edition.
pages cm.
Summary: An African wild dog, a warthog, a lion and an elephant argue about
the animal each sees through the hole in the wall—which turns out to be a mirror.
ISBN 978-0-8234-3535-7 (hardcover)
[1. Animals—Africa—Fiction. 2. Mirrors—Fiction.] I. Title.
PZ7.W64816Ho 2016
[E]—dc23
2015010970
ISBN: 978-0-8234-4522-6 (paperback)

A HOLE in the WALL

HANS WILHELM

I Like to Read®

HOLIDAY HOUSE • NEW YORK

A dog saw a hole
in the wall.

What was in it?

Another
dog!

The dog told his friends.
"I saw a hole with a dog."

The warthog didn't see

a dog.

The warthog told his friends.

"The dog is wrong. I saw a warthog."

The lion
didn't see
a warthog.

He told his friends.

"The warthog is wrong.

I saw a lion."

The elephant didn't see
a lion.

She told her friends.

The friends were
mad.

They all went to **the hole.**

And
they saw
a lion,
an elephant,
a dog,
and
a warthog.

Everyone was happy because everyone was

right!

The hole in the wall
wasn't a hole at all!

I Like to Read®

Betsy Ross
by Becky White • *pictures by* Megan Lloyd

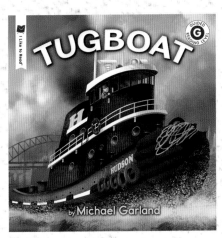

TUGBOAT
by Michael Garland

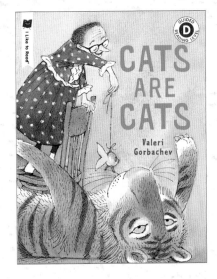

CATS ARE CATS
Valeri Gorbachev

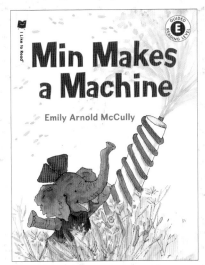

Min Makes a Machine
Emily Arnold McCully

BOOK
4

Family Album,

U. S. A.

JAMES
KELTY

CLASSROOM

VIDEO

COURSE

DRAMA CREATED BY
ALVIN COOPERMAN & GEORGE LEFFERTS

Maxwell Macmillan International Publishing Group
New York   Oxford   Singapore   Sydney
Maxwell Macmillan Canada, Inc.
Toronto

Maxwell Macmillan Canada, Inc.
1200 Eglinton Avenue E.
Don Mills, Ontario M3C 3N1

Cover Design: *BB&K*
Illustrations: *Duane Gillogly*
Interior Design: *Publication Services, Inc.*
Series Editor: *Howard Beckerman*
Editing and Production Supervision: *Ros Herion Freese*

Photo credits: All photos by Eric Liebowitz, except for screen lifts from video provided by The Dovetail Group, Inc., Cynthia Vansant, photographer.

This book was set in Optima by Publication Services, Inc. and printed and bound by Singapore National Printers. The cover was printed by Singapore National Printers.

Printing: 1 2 3 4 5 6 7   Year: 1 2 3 4 5 6 7

Maxwell Macmillan International Publishing Group
ESL/EFL Department, 866 Third Avenue, New York, NY 10022

Printed in Singapore

ISBN 0–02–332814–2

*C*ontents

ntroduction

Welcome to *Family Album, U.S.A.*, the exciting new American television series created to inspire English learning around the world. In 26 episodes, you will experience English in action and learn more about American culture. *Family Album, U.S.A.* is for everyone who has studied English for at least one year and wants to improve his or her understanding of the language.

Each television episode tells a story about the Stewarts, a typical American family living in New York. You will see the family in everyday situations, and you will share their many experiences as you hear English spoken naturally.

The unique format of each program includes the following:

PREVIEW   Before each of the three acts in an episode, a story preview sets the scene and introduces important vocabulary to aid comprehension. The preview usually asks a question for you to think about as you watch the act. Words on the screen help prepare you for the upcoming drama.

DRAMA   Each episode tells a complete story. In every drama, you follow the lives of the Stewart family at work or at play. Each episode centers around one important event, such as a holiday celebration, a job interview, a wedding, or the birth of a baby. The language level in the dramas follows a sequence. Grammar and vocabulary are simpler in the earlier episodes. In the later episodes, the language is more advanced.

FOCUS IN   After each act, a lively "Focus In" segment calls your attention to idioms, grammar, pronunciation, useful expressions, story comprehension, or important information about life in the U.S. The "Focus In" segments entertain you with music, animation, and humor as they highlight language and American culture.

Book 4 of this *Classroom Video Course* provides activities for Episodes 20–26 of the television series. On these pages, you will find a unique way to use the videos to study English. Each lesson follows this easy format:

PREVIEW activities correspond to the television previews.

VIDEO GAMES provide exciting scene-by-scene tasks for each of the three dramatic acts in a television episode.

FOCUS IN activities help you practice the points highlighted in the "Focus In" segments.

INTERMISSION and **FINALE** sections offer additional activities to help you develop language skills. These activities center around language and cultural points that are built into the television scripts.

THE CHARACTERS

Here are the people you will meet in *Family Album, U.S.A.*

MALCOLM STEWART	also known as Grandpa, 72, a retired engineer who comes to live with his son and his son's family in Riverdale, New York
PHILIP STEWART	Malcolm's son, 50, a doctor
ELLEN STEWART	Philip's wife, 50, a homemaker and a former music teacher
RICHARD STEWART	Philip and Ellen's older son, 30, a photographer
MARILYN STEWART	Richard's wife, 29, a salesclerk in a boutique and a clothing designer
ROBBIE STEWART	Philip and Ellen's younger son, 17, a senior in high school
SUSAN STEWART	Philip and Ellen's daughter, 28, a vice-president of a toy company, unmarried and living in an apartment in Manhattan
HARRY BENNETT	an accountant, 33, a widower who dates Susan
MICHELLE BENNETT	Harry's daughter, 9
MOLLY BAKER	a nurse, 43, who works with Philip in the hospital
ALEXANDRA PAPPAS	an exchange student from Greece, 16, Robbie's friend

. . . and other friends and business associates

"Quality Time"

In this unit, you will practice . . .
saying *I understand* and *I don't understand* in different ways
talking about literacy
reading a famous American poem

ACT 1

PREVIEW

SOUND OFF

1:00 - 1:44

Read the three summaries below. Then, with the the sound off, watch the preview. Which of the summaries best describes the scene? Can you guess? Circle *A*, *B*, or *C*.

A	B	C
Philip arrives home late and he's hungry. He is upset because Grandpa and Robbie had dinner without him. Robbie apologizes to his father. Philip tells Robbie not to worry about it.	Philip arrives home late and he's hungry. He is upset because Ellen left him only sandwiches and cookies for dinner. Robbie offers to cook something, but Philip refuses the offer.	Philip arrives home late and he's hungry. Ellen isn't home. While Philip has dinner, Robbie expresses concern that his parents have not been home for dinner lately. Philip says it is because their schedules are different.

Now, **with the sound on**, watch the preview again to check your answer.

VIDEO GAMES
Scene 1: "I wish I had her energy."
IN OTHER WORDS . . .

SOUND ON
1:45 - 2:52

Watch this part of the scene. What do the characters mean when they say the underlined sentences below? Circle *a*, *b*, or *c*.

1. Robbie: "I don't know how she does it."

    a. I am surprised at how much she accomplishes.
    b. I don't know why she didn't make dinner.
    c. I don't understand why she didn't come home earlier.

2. Robbie: "She sure keeps busy."

    a. She never gets bored.
    b. She is always doing something.
    c. She never forgets anything.

3. Grandpa: "She can't sit around and do nothing."

    a. She likes to be active.
    b. She doesn't like to sit down.
    c. She gets bored at home.

4. Philip: "My day was just fine. So was my night."

    a. I slept well last night.
    b. I worked a full day and part of the night.
    c. I can't wait to get to bed.

FILL IT IN

SOUND ON
2:53 - 3:09

Watch this part of the scene. Then read Ellen's note below. What words are missing? Write the correct word on each blank line.

_____,

WILL BE _____ LATE.

SANDWICHES IN THE _____.

AND COOKIES _____ THE _____.

_____ YOU _____.

_____,

ELLEN

Scene 2: "Our schedules are so different."

LISTEN IN

SOUND ON

3:10 - 4:51

Read the statements below. Then watch the scene and listen to it carefully. Which of the following items are true **according to the information in the scene?** Put a check (✔) in the box <u>only if you are sure the sentence is true.</u>

☐ **1.** Mike and Robbie went out to a movie tonight.

☐ **2.** Philip has eaten dinner alone every night this week.

☐ **3.** Philip is too busy to think about being tired.

☐ **4.** Ellen and Philip have different schedules.

☐ **5.** Philip is thinking about retiring soon.

☐ **6.** Philip will have a big breakfast tomorrow.

☐ **7.** Ellen baked some cookies.

☐ **8.** Grandpa is checking Robbie's homework exercises.

☐ **9.** Grandpa will go to bed soon.

BAD HABITS

Philip's schedule has led him to develop some habits that may be bad for his health and for his relationship with his family. Watch the scene again carefully. What bad habits do you see? Work with a partner to complete the sentences below. The first one is done for you.

1. Instead of coming home to have dinner with his family, . . .
Philip has worked late almost every night.

2. Instead of eating a hot meal, . . .
_____.

3. Instead of drinking something healthful with his meal, . . .
_____.

4. Instead of finishing his sandwich, . . .
_____.

5. Instead of spending time with the family after dinner, . . .
_____.

Scene 3: "You have that look in your eye."
WHAT DOES ROBBIE MEAN?

WITH THE WHOLE CLASS

SOUND ON

4:52 - 5:18

Watch the scene. Now read the three possible explanations below of Robbie's feelings about his parents in Act I. Which explanation best describes what Robbie means when he says his parents need more "quality time" together? Circle *A*, *B*, or *C*. Explain your choice.

A	B	C
Philip and Ellen should change their schedules so they can spend more time at home.	Philip and Ellen should do the things they used to do to have fun together.	Philip and Ellen should find a way to work together.

"QUALITY TIME"

SOUND ON

5:19 - 7:37

Watch the "Focus In" segment. Then watch it again and sing along. Here are the words to the song.

I got home late
After working all day.
I was hoping to find you,
But you were away.
You left me some dinner,
Something to eat,
But I won't be waiting up,
'Cause I've got to get to sleep.

I'm going to get home late
After working all day.
I know you'll be home,
But I'll miss you anyway.
I hope you find my note
And have something to eat.
I really want to see you,
But you'll be asleep.

We never seem to have any fun
Like we had before.
We're working too hard,
And I never get to see you anymore.

We have to make time for each other.
We owe it to ourselves and one
    another.
So why don't we do it?
What do you say?
Let's make some changes.
We could start today.

We need some quality time
    . . . together.
What we need is quality time.
  Oh, yeah!
We need to talk to each other,
Laugh with each other.
Let's get together, you and me.
With quality time,
We'll enjoy each other's company.

You're working long hours,
And you're never at home.
Sometimes it seems
You're just a voice on the phone.
And when you call,
You say you'll be home late.
You're always missing dinner
'Cause it just can't wait.

My job keeps me busy,
And I know you're busy, too.
I really want to spend
More time with you.
I'm getting up early,
And I'm coming home late.
If I want to see you,
I've got to make a special date.

We need some quality time
    . . . together.
What we need is quality time.
  Oh, yeah!
We need to talk to each other,
Laugh with each other.
Let's get together, you and me . . .

ACT I

INTERMISSION
GRAMMAR AND EXPRESSIONS:
Leaving a Note

A note is a written message to someone. To save time and space, writers of notes usually try to make the message as brief as possible. The note below could be much shorter than it is and still give the necessary information. Shorten the note by drawing a line through the words which are not absolutely necessary. If you can think of a shorter word for any of the words in the note, cross out the longer word and write the shorter one above it.

Dear Jane,

I have gone to the movies with the children. We went by bus. Would you mind picking us up at the Grauman Theater at 9:30? We will be standing in front of the theater.

By the way, Mona Seligman called us to inform us that the other car has been repaired. You can pick it up in the morning if you have time.

I left some sliced roast beef and potato salad in the refrigerator for you. You don't have to worry about washing the dishes that are in the sink. We can do them later.

Love,
Roger

USEFUL LANGUAGE

In Act I, you heard ways to . . .

- admire someone's accomplishments:
  I don't know how she does it.
  She sure keeps busy.
  I wish I had her energy.
- say you regret something:
  I feel bad about . . .

- state a general rule:
  It's not good to eat before going to bed.
- make an exception to a rule:
  A cookie can't hurt, though.
- talk about something that doesn't happen very often:
  They <u>hardly ever</u> see each other.

- ask someone's plans to solve a problem:
  What do you propose to do about it?
- say a person's expression shows his or her thoughts:
  You have that look in your eye.
  (= You look like you intend to do something about it.)

INSTANT ROLE-PLAYS

Practice this conversation with a partner:

At the office . . .

A: I don't know how he does it.

B: You don't know how *who* does *what*?

A: The boss. He keeps so busy but he never looks tired.

B: I know. I wish I had his energy.

A: You know, I've been very tired lately.

B: What do you propose to do about it? You have that look in your eye.

A: I'm going to start an exercise program and start eating more healthful food.

B: Me, too. Right after our coffee break.

A: Right. One last little doughnut won't hurt.

Then complete this conversation:

At home . . .

Husband: I feel bad about not spending more time with our son.

Wife: What do you propose to do about it?

Husband:

Wife:

Husband:

Wife:

Husband:

Wife:

Husband:

PREVIEW
SOUND ON

7:43 - 8:17

Watch the preview to complete the sentences below. Choose your answers from the Word Box. Write the correct word on each blank line.

WORD BOX
ought
how
committees
hard
alone
too
tries
to
have
spend
feels
late
time
away
think

What is Robbie's idea?

1. *In Act II, Robbie tells Ellen _____ he _____.*

   Robbie: Dad works _____, and he works _____. You work hard on all your _____, and you work late.

2. *Robbie wants his parents to _____ some _____ together.*

   Robbie: I think you _____ to take a vacation _____ from the family—_____.

3. *But Ellen knows that she and Philip are _____ busy _____ take a vacation. So Robbie _____ again.*

   Robbie: I _____ I _____ an idea.

VIDEO GAMES
Scene 1: *"You haven't been around much lately."*
IN OTHER WORDS . . .
SOUND ON

8:18 - 12:38

Watch all of Act II. Which word or phrase does Robbie or Ellen use to express the meaning of the <u>underlined</u> part of each sentence below? Choose your answers from the Word and Phrase Box. Write the correct answer on the blank line at the end of each sentence.

1. **Ellen:** What are you doing <u>awake</u> this late? _____

2. **Robbie:** You haven't been <u>at home</u> much lately. _____

3. **Robbie:** You and Dad <u>never see each other</u>. _____

4. **Robbie:** Well, you know how Dad is always talking about the kids in the ward and how important it is <u>to spend time with them</u>. _____

5. **Ellen:** I don't <u>understand</u>. _____

6. **Ellen:** As a matter of fact, it <u>is similar to</u> something I'm working on right now . . . _____

WORD AND PHRASE BOX

for them to be paid attention to

are like ships that pass in the night

get it

fits right in with

up

around

THE SUBTEXT

WITH THE WHOLE CLASS

SOUND ON

8:19 - 11:00

Read Ellen's and Robbie's thoughts below. Then watch this part of the scene again and listen to the conversation carefully. What do the characters say to express these thoughts? Tell your teacher to stop the tape when you hear each answer. Repeat the character's actual dialogue.

1

Ellen: You're not being honest with me.

2

Robbie: I feel like I don't have a mom anymore.

3

Ellen: The work I'm doing is more important than a vacation.

ELLEN STEWART'S SCALE OF VALUES

SOUND ON

10:24 - 12:38

A. Watch this part of the scene again. Robbie suggests the following two ideas to Ellen:

IDEA 1

Take a second honeymoon with Philip.

IDEA 2

Set up a reading program at the children's ward with Philip.

What do Ellen's reactions to Robbie's ideas tell you about her scale of values? Why do you think Ellen chooses Robbie's second idea?

B. Read the list of activities below. How would Ellen rate the importance of these activities to her? Write a number from *1* (most important) to *4* (least important) on the blank line beside each activity. Discuss your answers.

_____ rest and relaxation

_____ community volunteer activities

_____ family activities

_____ a personal hobby

"I DON'T GET IT"
"I GET IT"

SOUND ON

12:39 - 14:23

Watch the "Focus In" segment. Then watch it again and sing along. Here are the words to the song.

Ellen: I don't get it.

I don't understand.
    I don't follow you.
No, no. Oh, no, no.
    Run that by me again.
    'Cause I don't understand.
No, no. I don't get it.

Ellen: I don't get it.

What do you mean?
    I don't get the picture.
Huh? I don't get it.
Explain it all again
'Cause I don't understand.
No, no. I don't get it.

What are you trying to say?
What are you trying to say?
I don't get it.
Exactly what do you mean?
I don't follow you.
Could you explain that again?

Ellen: I don't get it.

I don't understand.
    I don't follow you.
No, no. Oh, no, no.
    Run that by me again,
    'Cause I don't understand.
No, no. I don't get it.

Ah, I get it.
    Oh, I see what you mean.
Yeah. I see what you're trying to
    say.
I get it.
Right! I see.
Oh, I know what you mean.
OK, I follow you now.
I understand.
I get it.

INTERMISSION

USEFUL LANGUAGE

In Act II, you heard ways to . . .

- say you don't understand:
  I don't get it.
  I don't follow you.
  Run that by me again.
  I don't get the picture.
  What are you trying to say?
  Exactly what do you mean?
  Could you explain that again?

- say you do understand:
  I get it.
  I see what you mean.
  I see what you're trying to say.
  I get it.
  Right!
  I see.
  I know what you mean.
  I follow you now.
  I understand.

- say two people don't see each other much:
  You and Dad are like ships that pass in the night.
- compliment someone:
  You are one fantastic Mom.
- give advice:
  I think you ought to take a vacation.
- make a suggestion:
  How would it be if . . .

IN PAIRS

INSTANT ROLE-PLAYS

Practice this conversation with a partner:

At the office . . .

A: Boy, my back is killing me. I hate sleeping on the floor.

B: I don't get it. If your back hurts, why are you sleeping on the floor?

A: The weather is cold.

B: I don't get the picture. You're sleeping on the floor because the weather is cold?

A: No, because the repairman didn't come.

B: The repairman? Run that by me again. A repairman has to fix your bed?

A: No. To fix my neighbors' furnace.

B: Exactly what are you trying to say?

A: The repairman didn't come to fix my neighbors' furnace. They're sleeping at our house because their house is cold.

B: Oh, I get it. You let them have your bed, and you slept on the floor. That's why your back hurts.

A: That's what I said in the beginning, isn't it?

Then complete this conversation:

At the office . . .

A: I'm going to quit my job. I have too many bills to pay.

B:

A:

B:

A:

B:

A:

B:

A:

B:

A:

READ AND DISCUSS

Read the paragraphs under "U.S. Life." Then discuss your answers to the questions under "Your Turn."

ON YOUR OWN

U.S. LIFE

It is estimated that one out of every six adults in the United States is **functionally illiterate**—unable to read and write for everyday tasks, such as reading the labels on food containers or filling out application forms. At the same time, more than 50 percent of all jobs in this country require more than a high-school education.

Adult literacy training is one very important part of the United States effort to provide its citizens with the skills necessary to become productive members of the work force. Many programs operated by schools and libraries across the country include courses designed to teach adults how to improve their reading and writing skills. In 1989, the First Lady, Mrs. Barbara Bush, became head of a national campaign against illiteracy.

IN SMALL GROUPS

YOUR TURN

1. Is illiteracy a problem in your country?
2. How old were you when you learned to read and write?
3. Do you think it is easier for adults or for children to learn to read?

PREVIEW

SOUND OFF

14:29 - 15:08

With the sound off, watch the preview. Then watch it again and pause at the three times below. What are the characters going to say? Can you guess? Circle *a*, *b*, or *c*.

1.

PAUSE AT 14:35

Ellen: a. The plan is an ambitious one. Read books with an advanced level.

b. The plan is a simple one. Involve the entire family in a reading project.

c. The plan is a funny one. Get a clown to read to children.

2.

PAUSE AT 14:46

Philip: a. My patients—mostly uneducated—wouldn't understand difficult stories.

b. My patients—mostly kids— would love to read and be read to.

c. My patients—mostly sad— would love to hear funny stories.

3.

PAUSE AT 14:55

Philip: a. Would you explain big words to the children yourself?

b. Maybe I should dress up like a clown.

c. Would you work with me on it?

Now, with the sound on, watch the preview again to check your answers.

VIDEO GAMES
Scene 1: "I couldn't agree with you more."
SPLIT DIALOGUE

IN PAIRS

SOUND ON

15:09 - 16:59

Watch the scene and listen to it carefully. Then work with a partner to complete the dialogue below. One of you will complete Ellen's lines; the other will complete Philip's. Watch the scene as many times as necessary.

ELLEN

1. Good morning. _____ a wonderful morning! Don't the flowers smell wonderful?
2. Did you find the _____ I made for you?
3. Philip, I've been working on this _____ project with the school board, and I'd like your opinion about it.
4. I've been trying to find a way to _____ reading.
5. Well, I think I _____ have found a way to do it.
6. _____ watching television. Well, that would be OK if, and I repeat, *if* people took the time to read.
7. The _____ is, how do we get them to read more?
8. I do have an answer, Philip. Or at _____ I think I do.

PHILIP

1. Good morning, Ellen. Yes, they do. That's why I'm _____ my paper and _____ my coffee on the patio this morning. Ah, it does smell _____. How was your school-board meeting last night? You must've come home very _____.
2. Thanks, dear. I was so tired I didn't _____ finish it.
3. What is _____?
4. Good _____!
5. Tell me about it. I work with families every day, Ellen. I see how people _____ their _____ time— young and old.
6. I couldn't _____ with you more.
7. I think you're going to give me the answer to that question. You have that _____ in your eye.
8. _____, tell me about it.

Now watch the scene again. Check your answers with your partner. Then practice reading the dialogue together.

Scene 2: *"The plan is a simple one."*

A READING PROJECT

WITH THE WHOLE CLASS

SOUND ON

17:00 - 18:50

Read the three summaries below. Then watch the scene. Which of the summaries best describes Ellen's plan in this scene? Circle A, B, or C. Explain your choice.

A	B	C
Ellen wants to encourage children to read. She also wants to spend more quality time with Philip. By working with Philip on a reading project at his hospital, she accomplishes two goals at the same time.	Ellen wants to start a reading program in the schools. But she thinks the idea must first be tested in another place. When Philip suggests the children's ward at the hospital, it seems like the perfect solution.	Ellen wants to start a reading program in the schools. At the same time, she wants her husband to relax more. She suggests to Philip the idea of reading in the children's ward so that he will spend some quality time there—apart from his usual duties as a doctor.

IN PAIRS

THE RIGHT ORDER

Watch the scene again. Then work with a partner to find the correct sequence of the lines of dialogue below. To show the correct order, write a number from *1* to *4* beside each line of dialogue.

_____ **Philip:** . . . Would you work with me on it?
_____ **Philip:** It can go beyond the school system, Ellen.
_____ **Ellen:** Maybe we can experiment with your patients and see how the plan works.
_____ **Ellen:** The plan is a simple one. . . .

Now practice reading the dialogue together.

Scene 3: *"And miles to go before I sleep."*

UNDERSTANDING POETRY

SOUND ON

18:51 - 20:39

IN PAIRS

Watch the scene. Then work with a partner to complete the exercise below. Take turns reading the statements. After you read a statement, ask your partner if it is correct. Write *true* or *false* on the blank line beside each statement. Your partner should then say one or more lines from the poem to support his or her answer. The first answer is given.

True or False?

____*false*____ **1.** It is not snowing very hard.
   "To watch his woods fill up with snow."

_____ **2.** The owner's farm house is nearby.

_____ **3.** The speaker is traveling on foot.

_____ **4.** It is the first day of winter.

_____ **5.** The speaker leaves because he feels cold.

"STOPPING BY WOODS ON A SNOWY EVENING"

By Robert Frost

WITH THE WHOLE CLASS

SOUND ON

20:40 - 21:31

A. Watch this part of the "Focus In" segment. Then watch it again and recite the poem along with the narrator. Here are the words to the poem.

Whose woods these are I think I know.
His house is in the village though;
He will not see me stopping here
To watch his woods fill up with snow.

My little horse must think it queer
To stop without a farmhouse near
Between the woods and frozen lake
The darkest evening of the year.

He gives his harness bells a shake
To ask if there is some mistake.
The only other sound's the sweep
Of easy wind and downy flake.

The woods are lovely, dark and deep,
But I have promises to keep,
And miles to go before I sleep,
And miles to go before I sleep.

SOUND ON

21:32 - 22:39

B. Watch this part of the "Focus In" segment. Which of the following descriptions explains the *rhyme scheme* (the way the poet planned the end rhymes in the lines of the poem)? Circle *1*, *2*, or *3*.

1. The first, second, and fourth lines of each stanza rhyme. The poet uses the last word of the third line as his rhyming sound for the next stanza. In the last stanza, all the lines rhyme.

2. The first, third, and fourth lines of each stanza rhyme. The poet uses the last word of the second line as his rhyming sound for the next stanza. In the last stanza, all the lines rhyme.

3. The first, second, and third lines of each stanza rhyme. The poet uses the last word of the fourth line as his rhyming sound for the next stanza. In the last stanza, all the lines rhyme.

ACT III

FINALE

ROBBIE'S POEM

After the reading program at the hospital got started, Robbie wrote a poem about his parents. With your partner, write the last word of each line of Robbie's poem. Choose your answers from the Word Box. Write the missing word at the end of each line.

"Quality Time"

Like two ships passing in the _____

My parents were never in each other's _____.

With paperwork, chores, and so many

_____,

They seemed to be living in two different _____.

I felt bad that they were never _____.

I wondered, "Can quality time be _____?"

Finding the answer was certainly _____.

But finally I said to myself "That's _____."

"Mom, you like reading, and Dad does _____.

Here's a goal you both can _____.

Read to the kids in the hospital _____.

Don't let them just sit around getting _____."

They took my advice, and now you _____?

The idea was a hit from their very first _____.

They found the solution in a simple _____,

And finally they're sharing some quality _____.

WORD BOX
tough
ward
night
found
bored
too
time
committees
pursue
show
rhyme
enough
sight
cities
know
around

READ AND DISCUSS

Read the paragraphs under "U.S. Life." Then discuss your answers to the questions under "Your Turn."

ON YOUR OWN

U.S. LIFE

Robert Frost (1874–1963) is one of the most popular of all American poets. Like Walt Whitman, another famous American poet, he wanted his poetry to be read and understood by "the common man." Frost wrote about farm and country life in early America, and his poems celebrate both the powerful force of nature and the strength and importance of human actions and choices.

IN SMALL GROUPS

YOUR TURN

1. Who is your favorite poet?
2. Reread the poem "Stopping by Woods on a Snowy Evening." What do you think the last stanza of the poem means? Does the reader know what "promises" the poet has to keep?

"A Big Fish in a Little Pond"

In this unit, you will practice . . .

       using *must have* + past participle
       saying indirect *yes/no* questions
       talking about career decisions

ACT I

PREVIEW

SOUND OFF

24:50 - 25:18

Read the three summaries below. Then, with the sound off, watch the preview. Which of the summaries best describes the scene? Can you guess? Circle *A*, *B*, or *C*.

A

Susan and Harry are talking about what their lives were like when they were Michelle's age. Susan says that life is very good for all three of them. She asks Harry why he has seemed unhappy lately. Michelle comes in and asks them if everything is all right.

B

Susan and Harry are talking about how they feel about their lives. Susan says that life has never been better, and she asks Harry if he thinks she should ask for a raise in salary. Michelle comes in and asks them if everything is all right.

C

Susan and Harry are talking about their lives. Susan says that things seem perfect. She asks Harry if he's going to tell her what is on his mind. Michelle comes in and asks if everything is all right.

Now, **with the sound on**, watch the preview again to check your answer.

VIDEO GAMES
Scene 1: "We couldn't ask for anything more."
IN OTHER WORDS . . .

SOUND ON

25:19 - 27:42

Watch the scene. What do the characters mean when they say the <u>underlined</u> parts of the sentences below? Circle *a*, *b*, or *c*.

1. Susan: "It doesn't need any alterations."
   a. It looks good without decorations.
   b. It fits well just as it is.
   c. It's warm enough without a jacket or sweater.

2. Harry: "She looks good in blue."
   a. I like to see her wearing blue clothes.
   b. She doesn't look sad in blue.
   c. She's happy when she wears the color blue.

3. Harry: "Michelle has been a different kid since we've been married."
   a. Michelle is happier.
   b. Michelle is not as happy.
   c. Michelle doesn't act the same.

4. Susan: "We couldn't ask for anything more, could we?"
   a. Is there anything else you want?
   b. We have everything we need now.
   c. We can't afford anything new.

5. Susan: It's good for every day.
   a. You won't get tired of it quickly.
   b. It will last a long time.
   c. It's a nice dress for school or play.

6. Michelle: "I always like skirts that go like this."
   a. . . . aren't too tight.
   b. . . . move around when you turn.
   c. . . . aren't too long.

7. Susan: "You had something on your mind when I said we couldn't ask for anything more."
   a. You didn't agree with me.
   b. You were about to say something.
   c. You didn't understand me.

8. Susan: "We must've bought the wrong size."
   a. It's clear that we bought . . .
   b. We need to buy . . .
   c. We didn't buy . . .

9. Harry: "Looks like we should've bought a bigger one."
   a. We had to buy a bigger one.
   b. We forgot to buy a bigger one.
   c. We needed to buy a bigger one but we didn't.

TWO-WORD VERBS AND PREPOSITIONS

Watch the scene to complete the sentences below. Choose your answers from the Word Box. Write the correct word on each blank line. Some answers are used more than once.

WORD BOX
over
on
up
into
off
around

1. Turn _____, Michelle.
2. Try _____ the skirt and blouse outfit . . .
3. Do you want to see the winter jacket _____ me, Susan?
4. Change back _____ your jeans, and put _____ the new winter jacket we bought today.
5. Come on _____ here, honey.
6. Can I take it _____?
7. Put it back in your room, and we'll hang everything _____ later.

Scene 2: *"That's a big decision."*

PAUSE

SOUND ON

27:43 - 29:34

With the sound on, watch this part of the scene. Pause at 27:50. What is Harry going to say? Can you guess? Circle *1*, *2*, or *3*.

1. I've been thinking, and I'd like us to have a baby.
2. I have been offered a job with a major accounting company in Los Angeles.
3. I have been looking at a new house for us in the suburbs.

Now watch the rest of the scene to check your answer.

LISTEN IN

SOUND ON

27:43 - 29:34

Read the statements below. Then watch this part of the scene and listen to it carefully. Which of the following items are true <u>according to the information in the scene?</u> Put a check (✔) in the box <u>only if you are sure the sentence is true.</u>

1. Harry has been offered a job with the largest accounting firm in Los Angeles.

2. Susan wants to move to a new city.

3. Harry has seven clients in New York.

4. Harry would be a sales executive in the new job.

5. The salary for the new job is very good.

6. Harry is going to get more details about the job offer at a meeting tomorrow.

7. Harry wants Susan to make the decision for him.

8. Harry won't accept the job if Susan doesn't want him to.

9. Susan would look for a job in Los Angeles if they moved there.

UNDERSTUDIES

IN GROUPS OF FOUR

SOUND ON

25:19 - 29:34

Watch all of Act I again. Work in groups of four to act out the scene. Three members of the group will play the characters: Susan, Harry, and Michelle. One person will be the director. The whole group should study the characters' actions and dialogue carefully, but it is not important to repeat the exact dialogue. Feel free to improvise—to change the words, to add new dialogue, or to add new action. Include the following information:

SUSAN	HARRY	MICHELLE
• comments on Michelle's new clothes: says how they look and fit	• comments on Michelle's new clothes	• models a new item of clothing for Harry and Susan
• expresses happiness at being married	• talks about how he and Michelle have felt since he married Susan	• interrupts Harry and Susan each time Harry is about to tell about his new job: asks if everything is all right and models more new clothes for them
• each time Michelle goes back to her room, asks Harry what he wants to tell her	• starts to tell her about his new job offer	
• reacts to the news of the job offer	• tells Susan about his new job offer	• comes back into the living room after Harry has explained about the new job offer and asks if everything is OK
• tells how she feels about moving	• says he won't make a decision about it without talking to her first	

Practice the scene with your group. When you can act it out from memory, perform it for the class.

Focus In

PRONUNCIATION

SOUND ON

29:35 - 31:39

Watch the "Focus In" segment. Then practice reading the following sentences aloud. Be careful not to stress (emphasize) the auxiliary *have*.

1. She must have been surprised.

2. They must have bought the wrong size.

3. She must have seen something.

4. She must have heard something.

5. I must have been crazy to come here.

INTERMISSION

GRAMMAR AND EXPRESSIONS: *must have* + past participle

Use *must have/must not have* + past participle to say it is clear that something did or did not happen:

The jacket is too small. We *must have bought* the wrong size.

You look tired. You *must not have slept* well.

Harry wrote the following note to his secretary, Alicia. What words are missing? Choose the correct verb from the Word Box and write *must have* or *must not have* + the past participle form of the verb on each blank line. The first answer is given.

Dear Alicia,

I can't seem to find the letters to our clients that you typed yesterday. I guess you _____**must have sent**_____ them out already. I also need the phone number of our new client, Mr. Ashora. It's not in your card file. You _____ it in there yet. Oh, well. I _____ it down somewhere. I'll find it. Also, could you order some more legal paper clips? I _____ a million of those last month! By the way, did Ms. Jefferson return my call yet? She _____ the message to phone me. How did I ever find such a great secretary as you? Thanks!

—Harry

WORD BOX

use
write
get
put
send

USEFUL LANGUAGE

In Act I, you heard ways to . . .

- **compliment:**
  I like it a lot.
  It fits well.
  I like the color.
  She looks good in blue.
- **say something that is clearly true:**
  We must've bought the right size.

- **say someone has changed for the better:**
  Michelle has been a different kid since we've been married.
- **express contentment:**
  I've never been happier.
  We couldn't ask for anything more, could we?

- **express regret:**
  We should've bought a bigger one.
- **be positive about a difficult challenge:**
  . . .we'll make it work for us.
- **say a situation is complicated:**
  There's a lot to think about.

↕

IN PAIRS

INSTANT ROLE-PLAYS

Practice this conversation with a partner:

Moving into the new house . . .

Wife:	You've been a different person since we bought our new house.
Husband:	I just love my new workshop.
Wife:	We're very lucky, the two of us.
Husband:	We couldn't ask for anything more, could we?
Wife:	Well . . .
Husband:	Uh-oh. I knew it. Well, what?
Wife:	I could use some bookshelves in the den. And now that you have a workshop . . .
Husband:	Shelves? Wow, that's a big decision.
Wife:	Why?
Husband:	It would mean that we'd have to move all the furniture out, and . . .
Wife:	And?
Husband:	And decide how many shelves, how big, and where to put them. There's a lot to think about.
Wife:	Maybe you'd better watch the football game on TV while I think about it.
Husband:	Good idea.

Then complete this conversation:

Three weeks later . . .

Husband:	Well, the shelves are all finished and painted. How do you like them?
Wife:	You do good work in your new workshop.
Husband:	
Wife:	
Husband:	
Wife:	
Husband:	
Wife:	
Husband:	
Wife:	
Husband:	
Wife:	
Husband:	

PREVIEW

SOUND ON

31:45 - 32:34

Watch the preview and pause at the three times below. What is Susan going to say? Can you guess? Circle *a*, *b*, or *c*.

1.

PAUSE AT 31:51

Susan:

a. Harry has been sent to Los Angeles to check on a job offer.

b. Harry has been wanting to move to Los Angeles.

c. Harry has been offered a job in Los Angeles.

2.

PAUSE AT 32:08

Susan: "There's Michelle."

a. I wonder if a move would be a bad thing for her.

b. I wonder if changing schools would be a bad thing for her.

c. I wonder if Los Angeles would be a good place for her.

3.

PAUSE AT 32:13

Susan: "And my job."

a. I don't know if I can quit my job so soon.

b. I don't know if I could make as much money in Los Angeles.

c. I don't know if I can get a good job in Los Angeles.

VIDEO GAMES

Scene 1: "A real dilemma."

IN OTHER WORDS . . .

SOUND ON

32:35 - 35:16

Which word or phrase does Susan or Grandpa use to express each of the following meanings? Watch the scene to find the answers. Choose your answers from the Word And Phrase Box. Write the correct word or phrase on the blank line after its meaning.

1. problem   _____

2. harmful   _____

3. a good name   _____

4. decide about   _____

5. things you do for someone else   _____

6. every now and then   _____

7. There's no good reason to wait.   _____

WORD AND PHRASE BOX

reputation

a bad thing

dilemma

sacrifices

from time to time

work out

No point in delaying.

LISTEN IN

Read the statements below. Then watch the scene and listen to it carefully. Which of the following items are true according to the information in the scene? Put a check (✔) in the box <u>only if you are sure the sentence is true</u>.

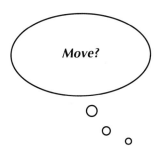

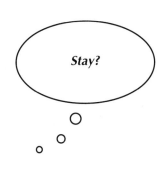

□ **1.** Grandpa and Susan are planning to have lunch together.

□ **2.** Susan is sure that a move would be bad for Michelle.

□ **3.** Grandpa says the final decision should be made by Michelle.

□ **4.** Grandpa thinks that every wife should make a sacrifice if her husband gets a job in a different city.

□ **5.** Susan calls Mr. Marchetta to ask him to find her a job in Los Angeles.

□ **6.** Grandpa thinks Harry has made the right decision.

Scene 2: *". . . a once-in-a-lifetime offer."*

SPLIT DIALOGUE

IN PAIRS

SOUND ON

35:17 - 36:19

Watch the scene to complete the sentences below. Then work with a partner. One of you will complete Bill York's lines; the other will complete Harry's. Watch the scene as many times as necessary.

BILL YORK

1. Harry, it's the _____ job for you. You'll love it.

2. She'll love it. It's a once-in-a-_____ offer, Harry.

3. The _____ is Craft and Craft, the biggest accounting company in the country.

4. The _____.

5. _____ it over. _____ it over. Let me know by the end of the week.

6. As soon as _____.

7. Let me _____ by the end of the week. It's a great _____ for you, Harry. _____ me.

8. Craft and Craft is the biggest in the _____.

HARRY

1. It's a big _____ for me, Bill. And I have to _____ it with my wife. I don't know if it's _____ for her.

2. OK. Tell it to me _____.

3. I know the company _____. It's *big*.

4. Yeah, yeah. The biggest. When do I have to _____ you know?

5. When would we have to _____?

6. I also have my daughter to _____. I don't want to _____ her school year.

7. I _____.

8. Yeah, I know. The _____.

Scene 3: "Did York make the offer?"

LISTEN IN

SOUND ON

36:20 - 37:50

Read the statements below. Then watch the scene and listen to it carefully. Which of the following items are true according to the information in the scene? Put a check (✔) in the box <u>only if you are sure the sentence is true.</u>

☐ **1.** Susan wants to talk to Harry without being interrupted.

☐ **2.** The job is Harry's to accept or refuse.

☐ **3.** Harry would receive a large salary increase.

☐ **4.** Mr. Marchetta promised Susan a good job in Los Angeles.

☐ **5.** Susan will work for Mr. Marchetta's Los Angeles company.

☐ **6.** Harry doesn't believe Marchetta will be able to get Susan a job.

☐ **7.** Michelle doesn't know about the job offer yet.

☐ **8.** Harry has decided to take the new job.

☐ **9.** Harry has a headache this evening.

WITH THE WHOLE CLASS

SUBTEXT

Read Susan's and Harry's thoughts below. Then watch the scene again and listen to the conversation carefully. What do the characters say to express these thoughts? Tell your teacher to stop the tape when you hear each answer. Repeat the character's actual dialogue.

1
Susan: I'm surprised. You don't seem very happy.

2
Susan: I'll sacrifice my job if it will help you.

3
Harry: I'm confused. I want to feel happy, but I don't.

ACT II

INDIRECT
YES/NO QUESTIONS

SOUND ON

37:51 - 39:58

Direct *yes/no* questions begin with an auxiliary before the subject. For example, Susan wonders,

> *"Can I get* a good job in Los Angeles?" (The auxiliary *can* comes before the subject *I*.)

Indirect *yes/no* questions begin with phrases such as *I wonder if . . .* or *I don't know if . . . .* After *if*, do not put the auxiliary before the subject. For example, Susan tells Grandpa,

> "I don't know *if I can get* a good job in Los Angeles." (The auxiliary *can* comes after the subject *I*.)

When a direct question begins with the auxiliary *do*, *does*, or *did*, the indirect question has no auxiliary after *if*. Study the examples in the box below.

DIRECT		INDIRECT
Do they want to move?	▶	I'm not sure *if they want* to move.
Does he like the offer?	▶	I don't know *if he likes* the offer.
Did she know about it?	▶	I wonder *if she knew* about it.

WITH THE WHOLE CLASS

A. Watch the "Focus In" segment. Then watch the segment again and pause at the four times below. Complete the indirect questions out loud with the whole class. Repeat the exercise until you can answer without hesitating.

1.

PAUSE AT 38:18

2.

PAUSE AT 38:44

3.

PAUSE AT 39:12

4.

PAUSE AT 39:37

IN PAIRS

B. Work with a partner. First you read the indirect question below; then your partner should restate it as a direct question. Take turns reading and restating the questions. The first answer is given.

1. I wonder if Harry wants the job.
Does Harry want the job?

2. I'm not sure if Michelle can make friends in Los Angeles.

3. I don't know if Susan will find a job there.

4. I'm not sure if Michelle has ever visited Los Angeles.

5. I wonder if Bill York offered Harry the job.

C. Work with a partner. First you read Bill's line below; then your partner should complete Harry's response. After you finish the exercise, switch roles and do the exercise again.

1. Bill: Is this job right for you, Harry?
Harry: I'm not so sure if _____, Bill.

2. Bill: Won't Susan love Los Angeles?
Harry: I don't know if _____, Bill.

3. Bill: Doesn't Michelle want to move there?
Harry: I'm not sure if _____, Bill.

INTERMISSION

USEFUL LANGUAGE

In Act II, you heard ways to . . .

- say you have a hard decision
  to make:
  It's a real dilemma.

- persuade someone to accept
  an offer:
  It's a once-in-a-lifetime offer.
  It's a great opportunity for you.
  It's the perfect job for you.

- introduce an honest statement:
  Can I tell you what I think?
  I'm not going to kid you.

- say someone else must decide:
  *It's something only you and
  Harry can work out.*

- offer advice:
  *In every marriage, sacrifices
  have to be made . . . from time
  to time.*

- say you shouldn't wait before
  doing something:
  No point in delaying.

- give someone a deadline:
  *Let me know by the end
  of the week.*

- refuse to rush a decision:
  *There's so much more to
  consider.*

- defend yourself for feeling
  or acting a certain way:
  How should I feel?
  I feel fine. Why shouldn't I?

IN PAIRS

INSTANT ROLE-PLAYS

Practice this conversation with a partner:

At the doctor's office . . .

Doctor: How do you feel?

Patient: How should I feel? I smoke a pack of cigarettes a day, go to parties every night, and I can still play a hard game of tennis the next day. I feel fine.

Doctor: Your tests are back from the laboratory.

Patient: What do they show? Tell me.

Doctor: I'm not going to kid you. Your blood pressure is too high. You should slow down.

Patient: Give up smoking and partying?

Doctor: It's a real dilemma. But, in every life, sacrifices have to be made.

Patient: You're right. I'll slow down, but not until after New Year's Eve. I could never miss the best party of the year.

Doctor: Can I tell you what I think? The way you're going, I doubt you will live to see New Year's Eve.

Patient: On the other hand, there's no point in delaying. I'll start today.

Then complete this conversation:

At the office . . .

Boss: I have the job offer of a lifetime for you.

Employee: What is it?

Boss:

Employee:

Boss:

Employee:

Boss:

Employee:

Boss:

Employee:

READ AND DISCUSS

Read the paragraphs under "U.S. Life." Then discuss your answers to the questions under "Your Turn."

ON YOUR OWN

U.S. LIFE

In the United States, as in any country, people who must decide whether to move to a different city to accept a promotion or a new job face difficult choices. Like Harry and Susan Bennett, they have to weigh many factors in making their decision.

At least Harry and Susan had a choice. Often, employers want to move an employee to a company operation in another city or another country. Then the only choice the employee has is between making the move or leaving the company to look for another job. During the last twenty years in the United States, many big corporations have moved their businesses from big cities to the suburbs, where rents are lower. The employees of those corporations have had no choice: If they haven't moved, they have lost their jobs.

Imagine the life of a professional baseball player. Most players are traded to another team at least three times in their careers. Some players (and employees of companies) insist that their employers sign a contract stating that they will not have to move for a certain number of years.

IN SMALL GROUPS

YOUR TURN

1. Have you ever moved to another city or country for a job? Did you have a choice whether or not to move?

2. Harry Bennett has to weigh several factors in making his decision: his own ambitions, his wife's situation, and his daughter's situation. Which of these factors do you think is most important to him? Explain your reasons.

ACT III

PREVIEW
SOUND ON
40:04 - 40:45

Watch the preview to complete the sentences below. Choose your answers from the Word Box. Write the correct word on each blank line.

WORD BOX	
family	feel
moving	about
kinds	decision
friends	wouldn't
job	talk
But	feelings

1. *In Act III, Susan and Michelle talk about* _____ *to Los Angeles.*

   Susan: How do you _____ _____ it?
   Michelle: Well, I really _____ want to move, but . . .
   Susan: _____?

2. *Later, when Harry gets home, Susan explains how she and Michelle feel.*

   Susan: Michelle and I have all _____ of _____ about leaving New York, the _____, and _____.

3. *Harry listens to them, but it's time for <u>him</u> to make a _____.*

   Susan: Now, tell us about your _____ with Mr. York. Did you take the _____?

Do you think Harry took the job?

VIDEO GAMES
Scene 1: "I couldn't agree with you more."
SPLIT DIALOGUE

SOUND ON

40:46 - 42:08

Watch the scene to complete the dialogue below. Work with a partner. One of you will complete Michelle's lines; the other will complete Susan's. Watch the scene as many times as necessary.

MICHELLE

1. I love my _____. I have so many good friends there now. I _____ miss a day even if I were really sick.

2. What's _____, Susan?

3. I know. I _____ you talking about it the other night when I was trying on my new _____. It's about moving to Los Angeles.

4. Well, I really _____ want to move, but . . .

5. But if you and Daddy wanted to, I _____ you know what's best for the family and for me.

6. I'd miss them a lot, but I know what it feels like to miss _____.

7. Does Daddy want to _____?

SUSAN

1. Come and sit down for a _____, Michelle. I'd like to talk to you about something. Something _____.

2. Oh, there's nothing _____, Michelle. But your daddy and I are talking about something that I'd like your _____ about.

3. You're _____. How do you feel about it?

4. But?

5. That's very _____ of you, Michelle. But what about your friends?

6. Honey, we don't have to move if you're not going to be _____ about it.

7. I think so. He's going to tell us _____ about the job offer.

Now watch the scene again. Check your answers with your partner. Then practice reading the dialogue together.

Scene 2: "Did you take the job?"
DID HARRY TAKE THE JOB?

ON YOUR OWN

SOUND ON

42:09 - 44:40

Watch this part of the scene. Pause at 43:23. Did Harry take the job? Can you guess? Choose one of the sentences below and finish it with your own idea.

1. Yes. Harry took the job because . . .

   _____

   _____ .

2. No. Harry didn't take the job because . . .

   _____

   _____ .

Now watch the rest of the scene to check your answer.

IN OTHER WORDS . . .

SOUND ON

40:45 - 44:40

Watch all of Act III again. Then read the dialogue below. Which word or phrase does Susan or Harry use to express the meaning of the underlined part of the each sentence? Choose your answers from the Word and Phrase Box. Write the correct word or phrase on the blank line at the end of each sentence.

1. **Susan:** That's very <u>thoughtful</u> of you, Michelle. _____

2. **Susan:** I see you're <u>feeling happy</u>. _____

3. **Susan:** Michelle and I have <u>mixed emotions</u> about leaving New York.

   _____

4. **Susan:** But if you think you should take the job, we <u>support</u> you.

   _____

5. **Harry:** I am so <u>affected emotionally</u>. _____

6. **Susan:** Harry, you didn't <u>refuse the job</u> because of me . . .

   _____

7. **Susan:** <u>What do you mean?</u>_____

8. **Harry:** I'm <u>important in a small organization</u>. _____

> ### WORD BOX
> all kinds of feelings
> touched
> turn it down
> considerate
> How's that?
> a big fish in a little pond
> are behind
> in a good mood

"A BIG FISH IN A LITTLE POND"

IN SMALL GROUPS

SOUND ON

44:41 - 46:29

Read the questions below. Then watch the "Focus In" segment. Answer the questions with your group.

1. How many offices does Craft and Craft have in the United States?
2. Name two advantages Harry has in being his own boss.
3. Decribe Harry's relationship to his clients.
4. What do Harry's clients say about his work?

FINALE

READ AND DISCUSS

Read the paragraphs under "U.S. Life." Then discuss your answers to the questions under "Your Turn."

ON YOUR OWN

U.S. LIFE

A "small business" is defined by the government as a business having fewer than 500 employees. In the United States, 98 percent of all businesses fall into this category.

Many small businesses are owned by one person. According to U.S. government statistics, of a total work force of about 100 million, over 15 million Americans can truthfully say, "I am my own boss." Almost 4 million of these **sole proprietorships** are owned by women.

IN SMALL GROUPS

YOUR TURN

1. Do you work for a small business? What are the advantages of working for a small business? for a large business?
2. Are you "your own boss"? If you're not, would you like to be? What are the advantages and disadvantages of working for yourself?

"Career Choices"

In this unit, you will practice . . .
using gerunds and infinitives as subjects
using idioms about confusion and finding a solution
talking about working mothers

ACT I

PREVIEW

SOUND OFF

1:00 - 1:40

With the sound off, watch the preview. Then, <u>with the sound on</u>, watch the preview again and pause at the three times below. What is Marilyn going to say? Can you guess? Circle *a*, *b*, or *c*.

1.
PAUSE AT 1:08

a. I've been trying to find a daycare center for Max so I can go back to work.

b. I've been wrestling with the question of whether I go back to work or not.

c. I've been wondering if you would take care of Max so I can go back to work.

2.
PAUSE AT 1:20

a. I want to continue my career as a designer, especially since I'm still young.

b. I want to find a good daycare center for Max, especially if he'll be there full time.

c. I want to be with Max as a full-time mother, especially when he's a baby.

3.
PAUSE AT 1:32

a. She wants to know when I think I'll be returning to the boutique.

b. She wants to know if she should hire someone else.

c. She wants to give me a raise if I come back right away.

| What does Marilyn want to do? |

VIDEO GAMES
Scene 1: "Rock-a-bye, baby..."
IN FACT

SOUND ON

1:41 - 2:28

Watch the scene and listen carefully to the lullaby that Marilyn sings. Then fill in the missing words below. Choose your answers from the Word Box. Write the correct word on each blank line.

Rock-a-bye, baby,
On the _____ top,
When the _____ blows,
The cradle will _____.
When the bough _____,
The cradle will _____,
And down will _____ baby,
Cradle and _____.

WORD BOX

come
wind
tree
fall
all
rock
breaks

Scene 2: "It's not the same, Richard."
IN OTHER WORDS . . .

SOUND ON

2:29 - 4:18

Watch this part of the scene. What do the characters mean when they say the <u>underlined</u> parts of the sentences below? Circle *a*, *b*, or *c*.

1. Marilyn: I've been <u>wrestling with the question of</u> whether I go back to work or not.
  a. unable to decide
  b. trying to decide
  c. asking everyone I know

2. Marilyn: And I'm <u>torn</u>.
  a. feeling bad
  b. angry
  c. uncertain

3. Marilyn: <u>It's not the same</u>, Richard.
  a. You, Mother, or Grandpa can't replace Max's mother.
  b. You, Mother, or Grandpa treat Max differently.
  c. You, Mother, or Grandpa are too busy to take care of Max.

4. Richard: That's what's <u>got you thinking</u>, isn't it?
  a. making you start to think about this
  b. on your mind
  c. making you nervous

5. Marilyn: . . . maybe she'll find someone else <u>in the meantime</u> . . .
  a. the same day I go back to work
  b. before I go back to work
  c. after I go back to work

WHAT DID SHE SAY?

SOUND ON

3:45 - 3:59

Watch this part of the scene and listen to it carefully. Marilyn reports a previous conversation. What do you think was the exact dialogue between Rita Mae and Marilyn? Write your answers on the blank lines below.

Rita Mae: _____ ?

Marilyn: _____ .

MAKE A MATCH

IN PAIRS

SOUND ON

4:19 - 5:04

Marilyn has mixed feelings about her situation. She loves her career, but she wants to be a good mother, too. Watch this part of the scene, and watch the whole scene again. Then work with a partner to complete each sentence below. Match the beginning of each sentence with the correct ending. Write a letter from *a* to *f* on each blank line.

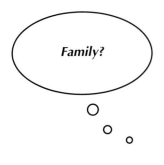

Family?

Career?

_____ 1. Marilyn's first goal in life has always been to become a top fashion designer, but

_____ 2. Marilyn would like to go back to work now, but

_____ 3. Marilyn could leave Max with Grandpa, Ellen, or Richard, but

_____ 4. Richard and Marilyn are trying to keep their expenses down, but

_____ 5. Rita Mae will probably allow Marilyn to stay home a little longer, but

_____ 6. Marilyn really wants to pursue a career in fashion design, but

a. she feels she should be with Max when he is a baby.

b. nobody can take the place of Max's mother.

c. sooner or later she will have to find a replacement for Marilyn.

d. in a way, being a mother is a career, too.

e. they really need two incomes.

f. having a baby has changed her priorities.

IDIOMS IN ACTION

SOUND ON

5:05 - 6:57

Watch the "Focus In" segment. Then watch it again and sing along. Here are the words to the song.

Marilyn: I've been wrestling with the question of whether I go back to work or not.

I'm wrestling with the question.
I can't make up my mind.
I'm in a fog. I'm up in the air.
I'm really in a bind.

I can't make my mind up.
I feel I'm split in two.
I'm pulled in two directions.
I don't know what to do.

I've got to get my act together.
I've got to get it all figured out.
I've got to get on the right track,
Get rid of all the doubt.

I've got to straighten everything out.
I want to try something new.
I've got to sort it out, think it out,
    work it out,
'Cause I don't know what to do.

Marilyn: And I'm torn. I really want to go back to work.

I'm really torn.
I'm all mixed up.
My future is unclear.
I'm pulled in two directions.
I'm practically in tears.

I'm of two minds about it.
I've got to think it all through.
I've got to find an answer,
'Cause I don't know what to do.

I've got to get my act together.
I've got to get it all figured out.
I've got to get on the right track,
Get rid of all the doubt.

I've got to straighten everything
    out.
And you know it's true,
I've got to sort it out, think it out,
    work it out,
'Cause I don't know what to do.
I've got to sort it out, think it out,
    work it out,
'Cause I don't know . . .
WHAT TO DO!

INTERMISSION

PRONUNCIATION: Stress on an Auxiliary Verb

You usually don't stress auxiliaries such as *am, was,* or *have* when they come before a verb, but to emphasize a statement you sometimes stress an auxiliary—to make your point more strongly. Look at the following examples.

> Richard: You've got yourself to think about, too.
> Marilyn: But I *am* thinking about myself.

> A: Will you please hurry up?
> B: I *am* hurrying up!

Work with a partner to complete the two-line dialogues below. Take turns reading and responding to each statement. Stress the auxiliary in your answer. Pattern your answers after the examples above.

1. A: You've got your baby to take care of.
   B: _____

2. A: They've got their own lives to worry about.
   B: _____

3. A: She's got her husband to consider.
   B: _____

4. A: You've got your career to think about.
   B: _____

USEFUL LANGUAGE

In Act I, you heard ways to . . .

- **express confusion or uncertainty:**

  I've been wrestling with the question of . . .
  I can't make up my mind.
  I'm in a fog.
  I'm up in the air.
  I'm really in a bind.
  I can't make my mind up.
  I feel I'm split in two.
  I'm pulled in two directions.
  I don't know what to do.
  I'm really torn.
  I'm all mixed up.
  My future is unclear.
  I'm practically in tears.
  I'm of two minds about it.
  Who knows?

- **talk about finding a solution:**

  get my act together.
  get it all figured out.
  get on the right track.
  get rid of all the doubt.
  straighten everything out.
  sort it out,
  think it out.
  work it out.
  think it all through.
  find an answer.

ACT II
PREVIEW

SOUND ON

7:03 - 7:42

Watch the preview and pause at the three times below. What are the characters going to say? Can you guess? Circle *a*, *b*, or *c*.

1.

PAUSE AT 7:08

Ellen: a. I've been meaning to ask you what you were thinking about regarding going back to work.
b. I've been meaning to ask you when you were going back to work.
c. I've been meaning to ask you if you plan to have more children.

2.

PAUSE AT 7:21

Ellen: a. I chose to give up my career as a music teacher.
b. I chose to continue with my career as a music teacher.
c. I chose to stay home and have more children.

3.

PAUSE AT 7:30

Susan: a. I have a job, and I have Michelle. I take care of both to the best of my ability.
b. I have a job, and I have Michelle. There are days when I feel like I'm pulled in two directions.
c. I have a job, and I have Michelle. I need both to make my life complete.

Watch the rest of the preview to check your answers.

What will Marilyn decide to do?

VIDEO GAMES
Scene 1: "I think I did the right thing."
SPLIT DIALOGUE

IN PAIRS

SOUND ON

7:43- 10:36

Watch the scene to complete the sentences below. Work with a partner. One of you will complete Marilyn's lines; the other will complete Ellen's. Watch the scene as many times as necessary.

ELLEN

1. There's your teddy bear, Max. He just _____ that teddy bear that Grandpa Philip bought for him.
2. Oh. Did he _____?
3. How did you feel? Tell the _____. Didn't you feel _____?
4. Helped _____? Or helped _____?
5. _____ of being a mother, I've been _____ to ask you what you were thinking about _____ going back to work. I know Rita Mae called. I can _____ what is going through your head.
6. There are so many things to _____. One _____ that makes it easier for you is that you have us. Max will always have a family member to _____ over him while you're at work. I didn't have that when Richard and Susan were _____.
7. I _____ to continue with my career as a music teacher. We _____ a woman to watch Richard and then Susan, and I continued with my career.
8. I think I did. But when Robbie was born, I decided to give _____ attention to _____ Robbie. I felt differently at that time.
9. Not exactly. I continued to _____ piano lessons at home.
10. I think I did the _____ thing for them and for _____ and for Philip. We needed the money. Remember?

MARILYN

1. I took him to Philip's office yesterday for a _____. You should have seen the look on his face when Molly gave him the _____.
2. No. My dear _____ boy just looked up at me as if to say, "Mama, what are they doing to me? Help!"
3. I sure did. I held him _____. I kissed the top of his dear little head. He looked up at me. He tried to _____. Being with him helped.
4. Being a mother is not easy, if that's what you _____.
5. I'm sure you _____, Ellen.
6. What did you _____ ?
7. Do you think you made the right _____?
8. And you gave up your _____ as a music teacher?
9. How did you feel about _____ away when Susan and Richard were babies?
10. Well, we do too, Ellen. Everything I _____ helps us towards _____ that house we want and need.

Now practice reading the dialogue together.

Scene 2: "That's what I said."
WHO SAID WHAT?

IN PAIRS

SOUND ON

10:37 - 13:52

A. Watch the scene. Then read the five lines of dialogue. Who says each line? Write *Susan* or *Marilyn* on each blank line.

1. _____ : We talk about <u>him</u> at dinnertime.
   a. Max   **b.** Grandpa
2. _____ : That is exactly what I wanted to talk to you about, Susan.
   a. your job   **b.** your marriage
3. _____ : Why does it have to be <u>one</u> or the <u>other</u>?
   a. your husband or your career
   b. your career or your baby
4. _____ : I take care of <u>both</u> to the best of my ability.
   a. Harry and Michelle
   b. my job responsibilities and Michelle
5. _____ : I don't know why I didn't think of <u>it</u>.
   a. working at home
   b. having two careers

B. Now work with your partner to decide what the characters mean when they say each of the <u>underlined</u> words. Circle *a* or *b*.

IN GROUPS OF FOUR

UNDERSTUDIES

Watch the scene again and listen to it carefully. Work in groups of four to act out the scene. Three members of the group will play the characters: Susan, Marilyn, and Ellen. One person will be the director. The whole group should study the characters' actions and dialogue carefully, but it is not important to repeat the exact dialogue. Feel free to *improvise*—to change the words, to add new dialogue, or to add new action. Include the following information:

SUSAN

- talks about Max and the toys her company makes
- persuades Marilyn that she can have a career *and* be a mother; explains how she handles her two responsibilities
- suggests that Marilyn do her dress designing at home

MARILYN

- asks Susan's advice about having a career but also being a full-time mother
- says she is going to call Rita Mae and invite her to talk about working at home
- expresses gratitude to Susan and Ellen for helping her

ELLEN

- tells Susan to relax
- agrees with Susan's suggestion; reminds Marilyn how she raised Richard and Susan
- suggests that Marilyn make dresses at home

Practice the scene with your group. When you can act it out from memory, perform it for the class.

GERUNDS AND INFINITIVES

SOUND ON

13:53 - 16:08

The subject of a sentence is sometimes a *gerund* (-ing) verb phrase.

EXAMPLE: *Being a mother* is not easy.

You can also say the same information by putting the word *it* in the subject position and by using an infinitive (*to* + simple verb) phrase after the main verb and its complement or object.

EXAMPLE: It's not easy *to be a mother.*

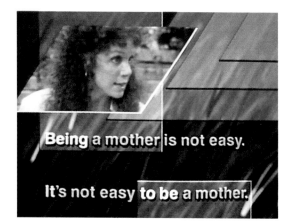

A. Watch the "Focus In" segment and pause at the four times below. Complete the sentences out loud that you see on the screen.

1.

   PAUSE AT 14:45

2.

   PAUSE AT 15:06

3.

   PAUSE AT 15:31

4.

   PAUSE AT 15:56

B. Now watch the segment again and sing along.

C. Think about the characters shown below. What do you think these characters enjoy doing most? With your group, write your idea on the blank line above each picture. Use a gerund or a gerund phrase. The first answer is given.

Fishing is my idea of a good way to relax.

_____ is my idea of a good time.

_____ would make my dream come true.

_____ excites me.

_____ would make me feel complete.

ACT II

INTERMISSION

USEFUL LANGUAGE

In Act II, you heard ways to . . .

- say someone looked surprised:
  You should have seen the look on his face when . . .
- introduce a question:
  I've been meaning to ask you . . .
- sympathize with someone:
  I can imagine what's going through your head.

- express anticipation:
  I can't wait till . . .
- say someone looks nervous:
  I've never seen you so wound up.
- talk about opposing things:
  My career as a fashion designer <u>versus</u> my career as a mother
- say you will do something as well as possible:
  . . . to the best of my ability.

- advise someone to accept an idea:
  That could solve your problem.
  I think that really answers your questions.
- express appreciation:
  I don't know what I would do without you.
  I'm lucky to have you all.

IN PAIRS

INSTANT ROLE-PLAYS

Practice this conversation with a partner:

Practicing the campaign speech . . .

Candidate:	"And, therefore, my fellow Americans, I will perform to the best of my availability . . ."
Campaign aide:	Ability. To the best of your *ability*.
Candidate:	Oh, right. "To the best of my ability." I can't wait *until* this speech is over. Speaking to the PTA always makes me so nervous.
Campaign aide:	I've never seen you so wound up. Relax. The PTA members love you.
Candidate:	They love me like mosquitos love a picnic. You should have seen the looks on their faces when I walked in.
Campaign aide:	Just remember to smile a lot.
Candidate:	How can I smile when I'm talking about raising taxes?
Campaign aide:	Why can't you do both? Tell them the taxes go to support their children's school.
Candidate:	Great idea! Hey, I don't know why I didn't think of that. It seems so simple now.
Campaign aide:	That could solve your problem.
Candidate:	I don't know what I'd do without you.

Then complete this conversation:

After the speech:

PTA member: We've been meaning to ask you about taxes. What do you intend to do about them?

Candidate:

PTA member:

Candidate:

PTA member:

Candidate:

PTA member:

Candidate:

PTA member:

Candidate:

PTA member:

PREVIEW

SOUND ON

16:14 - 16:53

Watch the preview to complete the sentences below. Choose your answers from the Word Box. Write the correct word on each blank line.

WORD BOX

course	full-time
wedding	disappointed
thought	would
kind	respect
decision	happy
plans	

1. *In the third Act, Marilyn tells Rita Mae about her _____ to stay at home with Max.*

    Marilyn: I've decided to stay at home and be a _____ mother.

2. *Rita Mae isn't _____ with the decision, of _____.*

    Rita Mae: I'm _____, but I _____ your decision.

3. *But then Marilyn tells Rita Mae about her _____ to design _____ dresses at home.*

    Rita Mae: What _____ of dresses _____ you design?

    Marilyn: I've _____ about that for some time.

    Rita Mae: Yes?

    Marilyn: Wedding dresses.

    Rita Mae: Wedding dresses?

VIDEO GAMES
Scene 1: "That's a good sign."
THE RIGHT ORDER

IN PAIRS

SOUND ON

16:54 - 18:30

Watch the scene to find the correct sequence of the following lines of dialogue. Work with a partner. To show the correct order, write a number from *1* to *12* on each blank line. The first and last answers are given.

_____ **Marilyn:** Welcome. It's so nice of you to come.

_____ **Ellen:** She sure got here quickly. That's a good sign. She must like you and your work, Marilyn.

_____ **Ellen:** Can I get you some coffee or tea or a cold drink, Rita Mae?

_____ **Rita Mae:** We met at the hospital. Hello. How are you?

_____ **Ellen:** I'm Ellen Stewart, Marilyn's mother-in-law.

_____ **Marilyn:** Oh, it's beautiful, Rita Mae! You shouldn't have.

12 **Ellen:** Well, I will leave you two to talk.

_____ **Marilyn:** I think she's just anxious to see Max. She loves children.

_____ **Rita Mae:** Oh, I just wanted to see your baby, Max.

1 **Marilyn:** That must be Rita Mae.

_____ **Rita Mae:** Hi, Marilyn.

_____ **Rita Mae:** My, how he's grown.

Scene 2: "Did you take the job?"

LISTEN IN

SOUND ON

18:31 - 20:48

Read the statements below. Then watch the scene and listen to it carefully. Which of the following items are true according to the information in the scene? Put a check (✔) in the box <u>only if you are sure the sentence is true.</u>

1. Rita Mae hoped Marilyn would return to work soon.

2. Rita Mae is not married.

3. Marilyn and Rita Mae have discussed the idea of custom-designed dresses before.

4. Marilyn wants both to design and fit dresses for customers at home.

5. Marilyn would also collect money from the customers.

6. Large wedding dresses are very popular now.

7. Marilyn will make a wedding dress for Rita Mae's niece, and then sell it after the wedding.

8. Rita Mae offers to take care of Max from time to time.

9. Marilyn has already finished some dress designs.

IN OTHER WORDS . . .

Watch the scene again. Which word or phrase does Rita Mae or Marilyn use to express the <u>underlined</u> part of each sentence below? Choose your answers from the Word Box. Write the correct answer on the blank line at the end of each sentence.

1. Rita Mae: I'm <u>anxious to hear.</u> _____

2. Rita Mae: . . . we can <u>increase business</u> to all kinds of dresses. _____

3. Rita Mae: It's a simple idea, and it will <u>succeed.</u> _____

4. Marilyn: It all <u>doesn't seem difficult.</u> _____

WORD BOX

work

all ears

sounds so easy

expand

ACT III

WORKING MOTHERS

SOUND ON

20:49 - 22:39

Read the statements below. Then watch the "Focus In" segment. Work with your group to determine whether each statement is correct. Write *true* or *false* on each blank line.

True or False?

_____ **1.** Marilyn's salary is used to buy food.

_____ **2.** Over one-half of all women in the United States with preschool children work.

_____ **3.** More mothers with school-age children are working than mothers with preschool children.

_____ **4.** Some grandparents take care of children whose mothers are at work.

_____ **5.** Daycare centers also take care of children.

ACT III

FINALE

READ AND DISCUSS

Read the paragraphs under "U. S. Life." Then discuss your answers to the questions under "Your Turn."

ON YOUR OWN

U.S. LIFE

Most married couples in the United States need two incomes just **to make ends meet**—that is, to pay for their monthly expenses. Such couples cannot afford to have one parent stay home to care for any preschool children. Many couples in this situation decide to place their preschool children in **daycare centers** that are **licensed** by the state.

Before states will give a license to a daycare center, the center must meet strict basic standards relating to health, safety, and education. Many daycare centers offer excellent recreational and instructional programs. Some people believe that daycare centers offer more than just an education. They believe that the social interaction provided by daycare helps these children to develop important social skills at an earlier age than children who stay at home.

IN SMALL GROUPS

YOUR TURN

1. Are you a working parent? If so, who takes care of your children while you are at work?

2. What do you think about placing preschool children in daycare centers? Do you think it is helpful or harmful to the children? What are the reasons for your opinion?

"The Community Center"

In this unit, you will practice . . .
talking about community action in the United States
using indirect information questions
using idioms about volunteering and group acitivities

ACT I

PREVIEW

SOUND OFF

24:50 - 25:19

Read the three summaries below. Then, with the sound off, watch the preview. Which of the summaries best describes the scene? Can you guess? Circle A, B, or C.

A	B	C
Grandpa reads in the newspaper that his friend Nat Baker was in a car accident. Nat is not hurt, so he comes to visit with Grandpa.	Grandpa reads something in the newspaper that he knows his friend Nat Baker is upset about. Grandpa invites Nat to the house to talk about it.	Grandpa reads in the newspaper that his friend Nat Baker is getting married. Nat comes to ask Grandpa to be his best man.

Now, **with the sound on**, watch the preview again to check your answer.

VIDEO GAMES

Scene 1: "He lives alone . . ."

IN OTHER WORDS . . .

SOUND ON

25:20 - 27:33

Watch the scene. Then read the parts of the dialogue below. What do the underlined words and phrases mean? Circle *a*, *b*, or *c*.

1. "The editorial in this paper has my friend Nat Baker real upset."
   a. The person who wrote the story
   b. The article expressing an opinion
   c. The sports story

2. "The old library building on Chestnut Street, which has been vacant for over a year now, . . ."
   a. empty
   b. for rent
   c. run down

3. ". . . was supposed to be made into a community center . . ."
   a. needed to be
   b. was expected to be
   c. might be

4. ". . . to serve the senior citizens . . ."
   a. college students
   b. older people
   c. voters

5. ". . . as well as the younger people of Riverdale."
   a. and also
   b. or
   c. and maybe

6. "Due to lack of funds for the repainting, . . ."
   a. Except for
   b. In addition to
   c. Because of

7. ". . . the plans for the community center have been postponed indefinitely."
   a. for a few weeks
   b. forever
   c. for an unclear period of time

8. ". . . it's set up primarily for kids to play."
   a. mostly
   b. first
   c. originally

9. "I never realized that."
   a. understood
   b. believed
   c. wanted

10. "It's hard for some older people to take all that noise."
    a. make
    b. tolerate
    c. hear

Scene 2: "Don't let me interrupt you."
LISTEN IN

SOUND ON

27:34 - 29:08

Read the statements below. Then watch the scene and listen to it carefully. Which of the following items are true according to the information in the scene? Put a check (✔) in the box only if you are sure the sentence is true.

1. Alexandra is better at math than Robbie is.

2. Robbie is failing math this term.

3. Robbie is graduating next Tuesday.

4. Grandpa is expecting Nat Baker.

5. Robbie drinks cola to help him concentrate better.

6. Grandpa didn't like math in high school.

7. There is a lot of math in engineering courses.

8. Grandpa did better at math in college than he did in high school.

9. Robbie is going to skip college.

Scene 3: "A serious matter."
SPLIT DIALOGUE

IN GROUPS OF FOUR

SOUND ON

29:09 - 30:22

Watch the scene to complete the sentences below. Work with three other students. Each student should complete the lines of one of the four characters: Grandpa, Alexandra, Robbie, or Nat Baker. Watch the scene as many times as necessary.

GRANDPA

1. That _____ be Nat.
2. I'd like you to _____ my friend Nat Baker. This is Alexandra Pappas, and this is my _____ Robbie, whom I think you've met once or _____ before.
3. Don't let us _____ you from your math tutoring, Robbie. I know you want to get to it.
4. I _____.
5. It _____. Come on out to the patio. We'll talk about it out _____.

ALEXANDRA

1. Sit down, Robbie. Let's _____ to work.
2. Nice to _____ you, Mr. Baker.
3. I told you. He'll use any _____ to avoid math.
4. What's the _____?

ROBBIE

1. Hi, Mr. Baker. We _____ before.
2. In town. At the _____ store.
3. _____ . . . _____.
4. Come on! You'll _____ about it.

NAT BAKER

1. _____?
2. I _____ now. _____. Hi. _____, Alexandra.
3. Did you read the _____ in the _____, Malcolm?
4. It's a serious matter for a _____ of us. A serious matter.
5. Thanks. Nice to meet you . . . _____.

Now practice reading the dialogue together.

NEWSPAPERS IN THE U.S.A.

SOUND ON

30:23 - 32:42

Watch the "Focus In" segment. Then watch it again and sing along. Here are the words to the song.

You can read it in the paper.
You can read what people say.
You can find it in the paper.
Most papers in the U.S.A.

Sometimes you can find good news.
Sometimes the news is bad.
Sometimes the news makes you happy.
Sometimes it only makes you mad.

But if you want to be informed,
Take my recommendation.
Go to a newsstand
And pick up a paper,
If you want information.

If you want to read the news . . .
    Look in the paper.
If you want an opinion . . .
    Look in the paper.
If you want to buy a house
    Look in the paper.
If you're looking for a job . . .
    Look in the paper.
If you want to buy a car . . .
    Look in the paper.
If you want to see a show . . .
    Look in the paper.

You can read it in the paper.
You can read what people say.
You can find it in the paper,
Most papers in the U.S.A.

If you want to know the score . . .
    Look in the paper.
If you want the weather forecast . . .
    Look in the paper.
If you want to see comics . . .
    Look in the paper.
If you have money to invest . . .
    Look in the paper.
If you want a recipe . . .
    Look in the paper.
If you need a vacation . . .
    Look in the paper.

You can read it in the paper.
You can read what people say.
You can find it in the paper,
Most papers in the U.S.A.

You can read it in the paper.
You can read what people say.
You can find it in the paper,
Most papers in the U.S.A.

ACT I

INTERMISSION

USEFUL LANGUAGE

In Act I, you heard ways to . . .

- **say something is hard to tolerate:**
  It's hard for some older people to take all that noise.
- **agree with someone:**
  I see what you mean.
- **express thanks:**
  I really appreciate you coming over to help me with my math.

- **excuse yourself for interrupting:**
  Don't let me interrupt you.
  Don't let us keep you from . . .
- **say you didn't understand something:**
  I couldn't get a handle on it.
- **remind someone that you've already met:**
  We met before.

- **talk about someone's dislikes:**
  He'll use any excuse to avoid math.
- **say something is very important:**
  It's a serious matter for a lot of us.
- **invite someone to a meeting to learn some news:**
  Come on. You'll hear about it.

↕

INSTANT ROLE-PLAYS

IN GROUPS OF THREE

Practice this conversation with two other students:

In an apartment . . .

Girlfriend: I really appreciate your coming over to fix my leaky faucet.

Boyfriend: Sure. Actually, there was something else I wanted to ask you . . .

Roommate: Oh, hi!

Girlfriend: _____, I'd like you to meet my boyfriend, _____. This is my roommate, _____.

Boyfriend: I think we met once before.

Roommate: Really? Where?

Girlfriend: I think it was . . .

Boyfriend: At a softball game.

Roommate: Well, don't let me interrupt you. I'm just on my way out.

Girlfriend: (*after roommate leaves*) What did you want to ask me?

Boyfriend: We've been going out for quite a while now, and . . .

Roommate: (*returning*) Don't let me keep you from talking, I forgot my car keys. (*leaves again*)

Then complete this conversation:

A minute later . . .

Girlfriend: At last, we're alone.

Boyfriend:

Roommate: (*returning*)
Girlfriend:

Boyfriend:
Roommate:
Girlfriend:
Boyfriend:
Roommate:

Girlfriend:

Boyfriend:

Roommate:

PREVIEW
SOUND ON

32:48 - 33:41

Read the six lines of dialogue below. Then watch the preview. Who says each line of dialogue? Write *Robbie, Nat, Grandpa,* or *Alexandra* on each blank line.

1. _____: We get our friends to roll their sleeves up and get to work.

2. _____: It's certainly a good idea. If I could take a look at the place, I could probably tell what it requires to fix it up.

3. _____: I can get some of my friends to go around the neighborhood and collect the furniture we need.

4. _____: And tomorrow morning, we'll all meet here to discuss the plan?

5. _____: Tomorrow morning it is.

6. _____: Where's your grandson Robbie and his friend Alexandra? Weren't they going to be here this morning?

ACT II
VIDEO GAMES
Scene 1: "I'll help."
MAKE A MATCH
SOUND ON

33:42 - 34:49

Watch the scene. Then match each job below with one of the pictures. Draw a line from each job to the correct photograph.

1. Supervise the refurbishing.
2. Find the people to help do the refurbishing.
3. Help in whatever way possible.
4. Get friends to collect furniture.

Scene 2: "If only Robbie and Alexandra were here."

LISTEN IN

SOUND ON

34:50 - 37:52

Read the statements below. Then watch the scene and listen to it carefully. Which of the following items are true according to the information in the scene? Put a check (✔) in the box <u>only if you are sure the sentence is true.</u>

☐ **1.** Joanne is a widow.

☐ **2.** Grandpa met Joanne once before.

☐ **3.** Abe is retired.

☐ **4.** Abe doesn't play with the jazz band anymore.

☐ **5.** Nobody knows where the two teenagers are.

☐ **6.** Robbie left the house early.

☐ **7.** Nat thinks Robbie and Alexandra weren't serious about helping.

☐ **8.** Abe isn't sure the building is strong enough.

☐ **9.** Grandpa will check the building on Tuesday.

☐ **10.** The building is dirty.

☐ **11.** The building has no tables or chairs.

☐ **12.** The community center will be designed for people of different ages.

WITH THE WHOLE CLASS

THE SUBTEXT

Read Grandpa's and Nat's thoughts below. Then watch the scene again and listen to the conversation carefully. **What do the characters say to express these thoughts?** Tell your teacher to stop the tape when you hear each answer. Repeat the character's actual dialogue.

1

Grandpa: I hope nothing bad has happened to Robbie and Alexandra.

2

Nat: Young people are too busy to think about community work.

INDIRECT INFORMATION QUESTIONS

WITH THE WHOLE CLASS

SOUND ON

37:53 - 40:07

A. A <u>direct</u> information question usually has an auxiliary, such as *were*, before the subject of the sentence:

What *were Grandpa and Nat* talking about?

In an <u>indirect information</u> question, after the question word *(what)*, use the word order for statements, not for questions. If there is an auxiliary *(were)*, it follows the subject *(Grandpa and Nat)*:

I don't remember what *Grandpa and Nat were* talking about.

SOUND ON

37:53 - 39:03

Watch this part of the "Focus In" segment and pause at the three times below. Complete the sentences out loud that you see on the screen.

1.

PAUSE AT 38:08

2.

PAUSE AT 38:30

3.

PAUSE AT 38:49

B. In a direct question with the auxiliary *do*, *does*, or *did*, the main verb is always in the <u>simple form</u>:

Where *do* we <u>meet</u> them?   Where *does* he <u>meet</u> them?   Where *did* you <u>meet</u> them?

When you change a direct question to an indirect one, do not use the auxiliary *do*, *does*, or *did*. In a question with *does*, the verb changes to the *-s* form in an indirect question. In a question with *did*, the verb changes to the past form:

I'd like to know where we <u>meet</u>.   I'd like to know where he <u>meets</u> them.
I'd like to know where you <u>met</u> them.

SOUND ON

39:04 - 40:07

Watch this part of the "Focus In" segment and pause at the three times below. Complete the sentences out loud that you see on the screen.

1.

PAUSE AT 39:17

2.

PAUSE AT 39:36

3.
PAUSE AT 39:55

ACT II

INTERMISSION

USEFUL LANGUAGE

In Act II, you heard ways to. . .

- say it's time to work:
Roll your sleeves up . . .
- say you will provide what is needed:
We might need you to come through with your friends.
- agree on a plan:
So we meet tomorrow?
Tomorrow morning it is.

- speak honestly:
Frankly, . . .
- say someone had good intentions:
They probably meant well.
- say someone got distracted:
They probably had other things on their minds.

- verify information you have about someone:
I understand you used to be in the construction business.
- confirm a statement:
A. You were in construction.
B. I was, indeed.
- say someone is acting strangely:
It's not like Robbie.

IN PAIRS

INSTANT ROLE-PLAYS

Practice this conversation with a partner:

After the party . . .

A: Did Paula and Don tell us they would stay to help clean up?

B: They did, indeed.

A: I wonder what the problem is.

B: It's not like Paula. She always comes through when you need her.

A: They probably meant well.

B: Yes, and judging by the way they were looking at each other, they probably had other things on their minds.

A: It's late. Suppose we clean this up tomorrow.

B: Tomorrow it is.

Then complete this conversation:

With Paula and Don after the party. . .

Don: The moon sure is beautiful tonight, isn't it?

Paula: Yeah. Say, I just remembered something. Didn't we promise to help clean up after the party?

Don:

Paula:

Don:

Paula:

Don:

Paula:

ACT III

PREVIEW

SOUND OFF

40:13 - 40:48

Read the three summaries below. Then, with the sound off, watch the preview. Which of the summaries best describes what is happening in the scene? Can you guess? Circle *A*, *B*, or *C*.

A	B	C
Robbie and Alexandra are late because Robbie got a speeding ticket from Detective Maxwell, a policeman. Robbie tells Detective Maxwell about the community center, and he comes home with Robbie and Alexandra to help out.	Robbie and Alexandra are late because Robbie met Mr. Maxwell, an architect. Maxwell lives in Riverdale and would like to help rebuild the community center. Robbie brings him home to attend the meeting.	Robbie and Alexandra are late because Robbie met Mr. Maxwell, a newspaper editor. Maxwell wants to support the group's effort to rebuild the community center.

Now, <u>with the sound on</u>, watch the preview again to check your answer.

ACT III

VIDEO GAMES

Scene 1: "We brought someone along who can help."

SPLIT DIALOGUE

IN GROUPS OF THREE

SOUND ON

40:49 - 42:03

Watch the scene to complete the dialogue below. Work with two other students. One of you will complete Robbie's lines; one will complete Grandpa's; the third student will complete Mr. Maxwell's lines. Watch the scene as many times as necessary.

ROBBIE	GRANDPA	MAXWELL
1. Hi, everyone. Sorry I'm _____. But Alexandra and I have been busy at work this morning on the community-center project. And we _____ someone along who can help. You remember Charles Maxwell, Grandpa? He's the _____ of the Riverdale paper. He _____ some nice articles on Mom when she was running for the school _____.	1. Yes, I remember. You _____ a great _____. 2. Let me _____ you, Mr. Maxwell. This is Nat Baker, who's_____ for this meeting, and this is Joanne Thompson—and Abe Lucas, who _____ to run the drugstore in town. 3. Let's go. What are your _____?	1. Hi, Mr. Stewart. Hope to be a bigger help on the new community-center _____. From what Robbie and Alexandra have _____ me, you people are making one big story. 2. Robbie and Alexandra told me what you need to fix up the old _____. I am planning to write an _____ that I think will help you. 3. OK. Now, I have . . . first . . . a couple of questions here. Have you talked to the _____ council? And have you had an _____ come in to do an _____?

Now practice reading the dialogue together.

Scene 2: *"What do you need most of all?"*

IN FACT

IN PAIRS

SOUND ON

42:04 - 43:33

Watch the scene. Then work with a partner to complete the list below. Watch the scene again if necessary.

1. Before painting the inside of the building, they'll need to:

_____

_____

2. Before they can start painting, they will need some equipment. They'll need:

_____

_____

3. Before actually doing any of the work, they'll need:

_____

_____

4. To start to furnish the center, they'll need (list six items):

_____

_____

Scene 3: *"Charles Maxwell lived up to his word."*

IN OTHER WORDS . . .

SOUND ON

43:34 - 45:01

Watch the scene. Then read the parts of the dialogue below. What do the <u>underlined</u> words and phrases mean? Circle *a*, *b*, or *c*.

1. "Charles Maxwell <u>lived up to his word</u>."
   a. wrote a great article
   b. writes as well as he speaks
   c. did what he said he would do
2. "The original plan by the council was <u>tabled</u> because of lack of funds."
   a. postponed indefinitely
   b. changed
   c. forgotten
3. "And it needs your <u>contributions</u> . . ."
   a. support
   b. donations
   c. used items

4. ". . . contributions of <u>furniture</u> . . ."
   a. tables and chairs
   b. dishes and kitchenware
   c. rugs, carpets, and curtains
5. ". . . furniture, paint, brushes, ladders, lamps, <u>et cetera</u>."
   a. if possible
   b. at least
   c. and other things

IDIOMS IN ACTION

WITH THE WHOLE CLASS

SOUND ON

45:02 - 46:29

Watch the "Focus In" segment. Then watch it again and sing along. Here are the words to the song.

Maxwell: OK, what do you need most of all?

Grandpa: People power. Men and women, young and old, to give us their time.

Pitch in, help out, volunteer!
Give your time, join in, lend a hand!
Pitch in, take part, we need you here!
We can do it with your help, yes we can!

We'll solve our problems one by one,
If we all work together, we'll get the job done.
Pitch in, help out, volunteer!
Roll up your sleeves, take part, we need you here!

Maxwell: What you're saying is, in order for this center to succeed, we need to put together volunteers from the various generations of future users.

PARTICIPATE! COOPERATE! COLLABORATE!
WE NEED YOUR HELP, LET'S GET TO WORK!

Pitch in, help out, volunteer!
Give your time, join in, lend a hand!
Pitch in, take part, we need you here!
We can do it with your help, yes we can!

FINALE

READ AND DISCUSS

Read the paragraphs under "U.S. Life." Then discuss your answers to the questions under "Your Turn."

ON YOUR OWN

U.S. LIFE

In this episode, Robbie, Alexandra, Grandpa, and Grandpa's friends volunteer their time to improve a community center. They plan to work together, without pay, to achieve a goal that will be good for the community as a whole. Cooperative spirit, or **volunteering**, has played a very important role in the United States. In the early years of American history, neighbors got together and harvested crops; built barns, houses, schools, and roads; put out fires; and helped each other during times of disaster.

Today, government—local, state, and federal—is expected to provide many necessary services. Yet because governments are increasingly hard-pressed to provide the high level of services that Americans are used to, community action groups and volunteers are more important now than at any time in recent history.

IN SMALL GROUPS

YOUR TURN

1. Have you ever participated in a community action project? Describe it to the class.

2. How important is volunteering to the society in which you grew up?

"Parting Friends"

In this unit, you will practice . . .
expressing regrets with *should have* + past participle
imagining with *if*
talking about American music and dance

ACT I

PREVIEW

SOUND OFF

1:00 - 1:44

Read the three summaries below. Then, with the sound off, watch the preview. Which of the summaries best describes the scene? Can you guess? Circle *A*, *B*, or *C*.

A	B	C
Robbie wants to marry Alexandra. Ellen suggests that Robbie wait a few years until he's older. Robbie wants to buy her an engagement gift. Ellen suggests that he talk with Philip.	Robbie doesn't want to date Alexandra anymore, but he doesn't know how to tell her. Ellen suggests that Robbie be honest and tell her the truth. Robbie says he wants to give her a gift.	Robbie is going to miss Alexandra, who is going back to Greece soon. Ellen suggests that Robbie give her a surprise party. Robbie also wants to give her a going-away present.

Now, <u>with the sound on</u>, watch the preview again to check your answer.

VIDEO GAMES

Scene 1: "Mom, give me a break."

LISTEN IN

SOUND ON

1:45 - 4:25

Read the statements below. Then watch the scene and listen to it carefully. Which of the following items are true according to the information in the scene? Put a check (✔) in the box only if you are sure the sentence is true.

☐ 1. Robbie is graduating soon.

☐ 2. Ellen is making baked potatoes.

☐ 3. Alexandra is coming to see Robbie before dinner.

☐ 4. Alexandra is returning to Greece soon.

☐ 5. Robbie would like to visit her in Greece.

☐ 6. Ellen doesn't think a surprise party is a good idea.

☐ 7. Robbie doesn't have enough money to buy a nice present.

☐ 8. Ellen will lend Robbie some money.

☐ 9. Philip is still at work.

WITH THE WHOLE CLASS

THE SUBTEXT

Read Ellen's and Robbie's thoughts below. Then watch the scene again and listen to the conversation carefully. What do the characters say to express these thoughts? Tell your teacher to stop the tape when you hear each answer. Repeat the character's actual dialogue.

1
Ellen: Alexandra is your girlfriend, isn't she?

2
Robbie: I enjoy being with her. I wish she could stay.

Scene 2: "I don't see any breaks or fractures."
THE RIGHT ORDER

SOUND OFF

4:26 - 5:20

With the sound off, watch the scene to find the correct sequence of the following actions. To show the correct order, write a number from *1* to *5* on the blank line beside each sentence.

_____ **a.** Philip does some paperwork at his desk.

_____ **b.** Molly leaves with the X-rays.

_____ **c.** Philip checks the X-rays.

_____ **d.** Philip gives the X-rays back to Molly.

_____ **e.** Molly enters the office with some X-rays.

Now, <u>with the sound on</u>, watch the scene again to check your answers.

Scene 3: "That's what fathers are for."
IN OTHER WORDS . . .

SOUND ON

5:21 - 7:36

Watch the scene. Then read the sentences below. What does the <u>underlined</u> part of each sentence mean? Choose your answers from the Word and Phrase Box. Write the correct answer on the blank line at the end of each sentence.

1. I <u>don't have enough money</u>. _____

2. <u>Everyone's in that situation</u>. _____

3. What <u>were you planning</u>? _____

4. It's nothing <u>attracting a lot of attention</u>. _____

5. I could <u>return the money to you</u> out of my lifeguard salary.

_____

6. I guess your mother and I can <u>afford</u> it. _____

7. You're <u>a good guy</u>, Dad. _____

> **WORD AND PHRASE BOX**
>
> **am short of cash**
>
> **pay you back**
>
> **manage**
>
> **OK**
>
> **did you have in mind**
>
> **flashy**
>
> **Who isn't?**

SHOULD HAVE + PAST PARTICIPLE

SOUND ON

7:37 - 9:54

Watch the "Focus In" segment. Then work with a partner to complete the activity below.

She *should have checked* the gas tank.

He *shouldn't have eaten* so much.

With your partner, think about things in your life that you wish you had done (things that didn't happen) and wish you hadn't done (things that happened). Use *should have* or *shouldn't have* + past participle in your answers. Write your answers on the blank lines below. Then say your sentences out loud to your partner. Look at the examples.

THINGS YOU DIDN'T DO

I should have finished college.

_____

_____

_____

_____

THINGS YOU DID DO

I shouldn't have put my bag of groceries on top of the

car; I forgot it and drove away!

_____

_____

_____

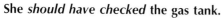

INTERMISSION

USEFUL LANGUAGE

In Act I, you heard ways to . . .

- object to something someone says:
  Give me a break.
- advise against something:
  Surprise parties don't always work out.
- express regrets:
  I should have saved some money.

- talk about gifts:
  I'd like to give her something to remember me by.
- agree to something if someone else agrees, too:
  It's all right with me if it's all right with your Dad.
- ask someone's opinion:
  What do you think?

- say you need money:
  I'm (kind of) short of cash.
- ask what someone is proposing:
  What did you have in mind?
- give and return a compliment:
  A: *You're OK, Dad.*
  B: *You're not so bad yourself.*

IN PAIRS

INSTANT ROLE-PLAYS

Practice this conversation with a partner:

On the phone . . .

Client: I'd like your advice about a financial matter.

Accountant: That's what accountants are for.

Client: There's a small beach house my wife and I really like. I'm thinking about buying it with a partner and his wife. What do you think?

Accountant: Hmm. Those arrangements don't always work out.

Client: What do you mean?

Accountant: Well, you and your friend may want to use it at the same times, or you might not agree on when to sell it. Then there's the maintenance to consider. Who will do the repairs?

Client: I see what you mean.

Accountant: Why don't you and your wife buy it yourselves?

Client: We're a bit short of cash at the moment. Oh, well. I'll think about it.

Then complete this conversation:

At the beach house . . .

A: What are you doing here? I thought this was our weekend to use the beach house.

B:

A:

B:

A:

B:

A:

B:

A:

ACT II

PREVIEW

SOUND ON

10:00 - 10:33

Watch the preview and pause at the three times below. What is the character going to say? Can you guess? Circle *a*, *b*, or *c*.

1.

PAUSE AT 10:06

Robbie: **a.** Would you like to come to a party?
  b. Would you be able to come over Saturday night?
  c. Would you come to a party Saturday night if I invited you?

2.

PAUSE AT 10:15

Robbie: **a.** My folks are going out for the evening and letting me have the house.
  b. My folks are buying the food and drinks.
  c. My folks are giving me a little graduation party.

3.

PAUSE AT 10:25

Ellen: Robbie, there's a phone call for you . . .

  a. It's Alexandra. She sounds upset.
  b. It's Alexandra. She found out the party's for her.
  c. It's Alexandra. She can't come to the party.

> **What's wrong?**

VIDEO GAMES
Scene 1: "I can't look at another number."

LISTEN IN

SOUND ON

10:34 - 12:57

Read the statements below. Then watch the scene and listen to it carefully. Which of the following items are true according to the information in the scene? Put a check (✔) in the box only if you are sure the sentence is true.

☐ 1. Robbie and Alexandra are studying math.

☐ 2. Robbie's eyes are sore.

☐ 3. Alexandra is flying to Greece on Sunday.

☐ 4. Alexandra accepts Robbie's invitation.

☐ 5. Robbie just got his driver's license.

☐ 6. Robbie's friend Mike is having a birthday.

☐ 7. Robbie will visit Alexandra in Greece.

☐ 8. This was Alexandra's first visit to a foreign country.

☐ 9. Robbie wants Alexandra to take his examination for him.

IN OTHER WORDS . . .

Watch the scene again. What do the characters mean when they say the underlined parts of the sentences below? Circle a, b, or c.

1. **Robbie:**   I can't look at another number.

    a. I'm tired of working with numbers.

    b. My eyes hurt from looking at numbers.

    c. I don't like numbers.

2. **Robbie:**   Oh, by the way, when is your plane reservation for your flight to Athens?

    a. I'm not sure

    b. I just remembered to ask

    c. when you're traveling

3. **Robbie:**   It's a date.

    a. OK. It's all settled.

    b. That's a good idea.

    c. What a surprise.

4. **Alexandra:**   You've been like a second family to me.

    a. a replacement for my own family

    b. almost as good as my own family

    c. better than my own family

Scene 2: "I have to run."
PAUSE

SOUND ON
12:58 - 13:21

With the sound on, watch this part of the scene and pause at 13:13. What will happen next? Can you guess? Circle A, B, or C, or any combination of A, B, and C.

A	B	C
Robbie and Alexandra kiss.	Alexandra wishes Robbie "Good Luck" on the test.	The sound of a car horn is heard in the driveway.

Now watch the rest of the scene to check your answer.

Scene 3: "You are going to miss her."
HOW DOES ROBBIE FEEL?

WITH THE WHOLE CLASS

SOUND ON
13:22 - 13:58

Read the three possible explanations below of Robbie's feelings about Alexandra. Then watch the scene. Think about Robbie's past conversations with Alexandra. Which explanation below best describes Robbie's feelings? Circle A, B, or C. Explain your choice.

A	B	C
Robbie is not sure how he feels about Alexandra. He's not sure if he'll miss her or not.	Robbie will miss Alexandra because she is a good friend. She often helps him with his math.	Robbie will miss Alexandra a lot. She is his first girlfriend.

Scene 4: "You what? Oh, no!"

ON CUE

IN PAIRS

SOUND OFF

13:59 - 15:08

With the sound off, watch the scene. Then read the first line below that Robbie says. What do you think Sandra says before Robbie's line? Can you guess? Work with a partner. Write your idea or ideas on the blank line beside Sandra's name. Then try to guess Mike's and Ellen's lines.

1. **Sandra:** _____ ?
   Robbie: Absolutely. She has no idea that the party is in her honor.

2. **Mike:** _____ ?
   Millie: They're in my bag.

3. **Mike:** _____ ?
   Millie: Some rock 'n' roll.

4. **Mike:** _____ ?
   Robbie: My mom's decorating it right now.

5. **Ellen:** _____ ?
   Robbie: OK. Thanks, Mom. I'll take it in there.

Now, <u>with the sound on</u>, watch the scene to check your answers.

Focus In

IMAGINING WITH *IF*

IN SMALL GROUPS

SOUND ON

15:09 - 17:00

A. Watch the "Focus In" segment. Then work in small groups. Together, try to explain the grammar rules for imagining about the present or the future. Which verb form do you use after *if*? Which auxiliaries can you use before the main verb?

B. Now use your imagination. Work with your group to finish the sentences below with ideas of your own. Think of more than one idea for each sentence.

1. If today were the last day of school, _____.
   _____.

2. If airline travel were free, _____.
   _____.

3. If all people spoke the same language, _____.
   _____.

4. If I governed the world, _____.
   _____.

5. If plants and animals could speak, _____.
   _____.

ACT II

INTERMISSION

USEFUL LANGUAGE

In Act II, you heard ways to . . .

- **introduce a statement:**
  You know what?
  By the way, . . .
- **say you're tired of something:**
  I can't look at another . . .
- **refuse an offer:**
  That isn't necessary.

- **accept an offer:**
  That would be very nice.
- **confirm an engagement:**
  It's a date.
- **express appreciation:**
  You've been like a second family to me.
- **imagine:**
  Wouldn't it be nice if . . .

- **ask if someone can go somewhere alone:**
  Will you be all right?
- **say you can't replace something:**
  It's not the same.
- **say an event is a celebration for someone:**
  The party is in her honor.
- **say you'll go to a phone to accept a call:**
  I'll take it in there.

IN PAIRS

INSTANT ROLE-PLAYS

Practice this conversation with a partner:

With a good friend . . .

Friend: Ready for the next one?

You: Sorry, I can't look at another math problem right now.

Friend: How about the last problem? That looks easy.

You: I would rather do the English assignment.

Friend: It would be nice if we could skip the math and get right to the English, but we can't.

You: But homework is homework.

Friend: It's not the same. The math is due tomorrow; the English isn't due until next week.

You: You know what?

Friend: What?

You: I have two tickets to a rock 'n' roll concert. Would you like to go?

Friend: When?

You: Saturday night.

Friend: It's a date.

Then complete this conversation:

At the concert . . .

You: Isn't this a great concert?

Friend:

You:

Friend:

You:

Friend:

You:

Friend:

You:

Friend:

You:

Friend:

You:

PREVIEW
SOUND OFF

17:06 - 17:47

Read the three summaries below. Then, with the sound off, watch the preview. Which summary best describes the preview? Can you guess? Circle A, B, or C.

A	B	C
Alexandra can't come to the party because her flight tomorrow was canceled and she has to take an earlier one today.	Alexandra can't come to the party because the Molinas are giving her a going-away party.	Alexandra isn't coming to the party because she found out the party is for her and is too shy to be the guest of honor.

Now, with the sound on, watch the preview to check your answer.

VIDEO GAMES
Scene 1: "Well, that must be him."
SPLIT DIALOGUE

IN GROUPS OF FOUR

SOUND ON

17:48 - 18:38

Watch the scene and listen to it carefully. Each member of your group should complete the dialogue for one of the characters. Watch the scene as many times as necessary.

MILLIE

1. How _____ some music?
2. Did she _____ why she had to _____ today?
3. This is _____.

ROBBIE

1. OK, I guess. Especially _____ Alexandra gave me a _____ . . .
2. _____!

MIKE

1. She _____ Robbie that her flight tomorrow was _____ so she had to take an _____ flight today.
2. Well, that must be him.
3. I don't know. _____ he's angry.
4. Too _____ now. We _____ have done it sooner. Oh, _____ he comes.
5. Hi! How'd it go?
6. Yeah? _____ was it?

SANDRA

1. No, let's _____ till Robbie gets _____ from the airport.
2. Why is he blowing his _____ like that?
3. Do you think we should _____ down the decorations? They'll just _____ him sad.

Check your answers with your group.

FREEZE!

WITH THE WHOLE CLASS

PAUSE AT 18:38

What is Alexandra's surprise? Tell your opinions. You will find out the answer in the next scene!

Scene 2: "Hear, hear!"

UNDERSTUDIES

IN GROUPS OF FOUR

SOUND ON

18:39 - 20:46

Watch this part of the scene and listen to it carefully. Work in groups of four to act out the scene. One student will be the director; the director will also play the parts of both Philip and Mike. One student will play the parts of Sandra, Millie, and Ellen. The other two students will play Alexandra and Robbie. The whole group should study the characters' actions and dialogue carefully, but it is not important to repeat the exact dialogue. Feel free to *improvise*—to change the words, to add new dialogue, or to add new action. Include the following information:

SANDRA	**ALEXANDRA**	**MIKE**	**ROBBIE**
• gives Alexandra a hug and asks what happened	• explains about her phone call to her parents and her flight home Monday	• expresses excitement that Alexandra is here	• expresses thanks to Alexandra and says she's a real friend
• asks Alexandra how she knew the party was for her	• says that Robbie explained about the party and shows the gift he gave her	• suggests starting the music	• opens Alexandra's present to him and reads the inscription
MILLIE	• asks everyone if she can say something	**PHILIP**	• expresses surprise that the gifts are the same
• invites everyone to start the party now	• expresses thanks to Robbie and the Stewart family	• says "Hear, hear!"	• asks Alexandra to dance with him
• expresses admiration for Alexandra's gift	• gives Robbie her going-away present to him	• asks Ellen to dance with him	
ELLEN			
• accepts Philip's offer to dance			

"I'M GOING TO MISS YOU"

WITH THE WHOLE CLASS

SOUND ON

20:47 - 22:38

Watch the "Focus In" segment. Then play it again and sing along. Here are the words to the song.

You've become my friend,
Though I haven't known you very long.
You've always made me feel so right at home.

You've become my friend.
I can always be myself with you,
And when I think of you I'm not alone.

You've become my friend.
You were always there when I needed you.
Never had to ask for anything.
You were there to help me through.

I'll remember all the times
That we spent together having fun.
I won't forget a moment that we shared.

I won't forget your smile,
Won't forget the way you made me laugh,
The things you did to show me that you care.

I'm going to miss you.
I'm going to miss you.
It's hard to say good-bye 'cause you're my friend.

I'm going to miss you.
Yes, I'm going to miss you.
But sometime in the future—
We don't know where or when—
We'll be saying "hello" again.

FINALE

READ AND DISCUSS

Read the paragraphs under "U.S. Life." Then discuss your answers to the questions under "Your Turn."

ON YOUR OWN

U.S. LIFE

At Alexandra's party, Philip and Ellen do not dance the same way as Robbie, Alexandra, and their friends. Robbie's parents are dancing in a style that became popular in the 1940s. During this period, the "big bands"—orchestras led by such famous people as Benny Goodman and Tommy Dorsey—dominated the popular music scene. The music emphasized harmony and repeated melodies; the dancing, like the music, was smooth.

When rock 'n' roll music became popular in the late 1950s, it was accompanied by a great variety of energetic dance styles. The idea was to "move to the music" any way you felt like moving. Popular dance has become more and more free since that time.

IN SMALL GROUPS

YOUR TURN

1. Do you like to dance? What is your favorite style of music to dance to?

2. Describe some of the dance styles of your country—traditional and contemporary.

3. Is there a big difference in the way your parents' generation danced and the way you dance?

"Country Music"

In this unit, you will practice . . .
using the present tense with future meaning
expressing past "unreal" wishes and conditions
talking about camping

ACT 1

PREVIEW

SOUND OFF

24:50 - 25:32

Read the three summaries below. Then, with the sound off, watch the preview. Which summary best describes the preview? Circle *A*, *B*, or *C*.

A	B	C
Richard and Marilyn are going on a camping trip. They want to bring Max, so Ellen will also come along to do the babysitting. Marilyn is upset because she thinks Max is too young to sleep outside in a tent.	Richard and Marilyn are going on a camping trip. Max is too young to go, so Ellen has offered to babysit while they are away. Marilyn is upset because she thinks Max needs his mother to take care of him.	Richard and Marilyn are going on a camping trip. Max is too young to go, so Ellen has offered to babysit while they are away. Marilyn is upset because she doesn't want to leave Ellen with the responsibility of taking care of Max.

Now, with the sound on, watch the preview to check your answer.

VIDEO GAMES
Scene 1: "Hot dogs and mustard."
LISTEN IN

SOUND ON

25:33 - 28:39

Read the statements below. Then watch the scene and listen to it carefully. Which of the following items are true according to the information in the scene? Put a check (✔) in the box only if you are sure the sentence is true.

☐ **1.** Richard likes American hot dogs better than anything else.

☐ **2.** The Stewarts had picnics at the beach years ago.

☐ **3.** Richard doesn't like mustard on his hot dogs.

☐ **4.** Richard and Marilyn are leaving today.

☐ **5.** Ellen will take care of Max while Richard and Marilyn are away.

☐ **6.** Harry and Susan are bringing Michelle along on the camping trip.

☐ **7.** Max is getting his first teeth.

☐ **8.** Marilyn is worried that taking care of Max will be too much work for Ellen.

☐ **9.** Philip is not going on the camping trip.

☐ **10.** Max feels better when he lies face down.

☐ **11.** The camping trip will include Saturday, Saturday night, and Sunday.

☐ **12.** Richard will telephone Ellen to make sure everything is all right.

IN OTHER WORDS . . .

Watch the scene again. Who or what are the characters referring to when they use each of the underlined pronouns below? Write your answer on the blank line at the end of each sentence.

1. Richard: I wish I had one now. _____

2. Richard: I have to remember to put them in the bag tomorrow morning before we leave. _____

3. Ellen: It's no big deal. I am happy to do it for you. _____

4. Marilyn: I wish he felt better. _____

Scene 2: "I hope he's good when we're away."
CAMPING CHECKLIST

SOUND ON

25:33 - 29:51

Watch the scene. What items are Richard and Marilyn taking on their camping trip? Put a check (✔) on the blank line beside each correct item below.

_____ **1.** flashlight

_____ **2.** beach ball

_____ **3.** bottle opener

_____ **4.** sleeping bag

_____ **5.** mosquito repellent

_____ **6.** matches

_____ **7.** newspaper

_____ **8.** long underwear

_____ **9.** umbrella

_____ **10.** camera and film

_____ **11.** radio

_____ **12.** cassette player

_____ **13.** raincoat

_____ **14.** air mattress

_____ **15.** tent

IN OTHER WORDS . . .

SOUND ON

28:40 - 29:51

Watch all of Act I again. Which word or phrase do the characters use to express the meaning of the <u>underlined</u> part of each sentence below? Choose your answers from the Word and Phrase Box. Write the correct answer on the blank line at the end of each sentence.

1. Richard: I might as well take it <u>with us</u>. _____

2. Ellen: It's <u>not important</u>. _____

3. Ellen: He's <u>getting his first teeth</u>. _____

4. Richard: We really don't have to be <u>very worried</u>.

_____

5. Ellen: You're going to have <u>a wonderful trip</u>.

_____

6. Marilyn: I hope he <u>behaves well</u> when we're away. _____

7. Richard: And we're bringing the ketchup, mustard, relish—all

<u>those things</u>. _____

WORD AND PHRASE BOX

the time of your lives

is good

no big deal

along

that stuff

teething

overly concerned

PRESENT TENSE WITH FUTURE MEANING

SOUND ON

29:52 - 32:08

Watch the "Focus In" segment. Then complete the sentences below by filling in each blank line with the correct form of a verb from the Word Box.

1. Marilyn is a good mother. She goes to Max as soon as he _____ .

2. Philip is a doctor. He'll take care of Max if there _____ a medical problem.

3. Marilyn and Richard are all packed. They'll be ready when Harry and Susan _____ tomorrow.

4. Richard will make sure they have everything on the list before they _____ tomorrow.

5. Marilyn will rub Max's back until he _____ to sleep.

6. Richard will continue packing while Marilyn _____ care of Max.

WORD BOX

go

arrive

take

be

cry

leave

will be away

when we're away

ACT I

INTERMISSION

USEFUL LANGUAGE

In Act I, you heard ways to . . .

- express a strong appreciation:
  There's nothing like a hot dog in the country.
- say there's no reason not to do something:
  I might as well take it along.

- lessen the importance of something:
  It's no big deal.
  It's only one night.
- say someone is going to have a wonderful time:
  You're going to have the time of your lives.

- express concern:
  I'm really concerned about . . .
  I'm still worried about you, Ellen.
- say you're glad to do something for somebody:
  It will be my great pleasure . . .

IN GROUPS OF THREE

INSTANT ROLE-PLAYS

Practice this conversation with two partners:

At home before the weekend vacation . . .

Mom: I'm really concerned about leaving you all alone for the weekend.

Son: Don't worry, Mom. It's only for the weekend. I'll be fine.

Dad: This will be your first time on your own.

Son: It's no big deal, Dad. Really.

Mom: Remember what we talked about? No parties while we're gone.

Son: As soon as you leave, this place will be as quiet as a cemetery.

Dad: I still don't feel right about leaving you alone.

Son: Go on, Dad. You and Mom are going to have the time of your lives.

Then complete this conversation:

That night, as Mom and Dad arrive back in front of the house unexpectedly . . .

Dad: Well, it's too bad the trip was canceled.

Mom: Yes. Say, all the lights in the house are on.

Dad: And what's all that noise?

As they enter the house and find a party going on . . .

Dad:

Son:

Mom:

Son:

Dad:

Son:

Mom:

Son:

PREVIEW

SOUND ON

32:14 - 33:01

Watch the preview to complete the sentences below. Choose your answers from the Word Box. Write the correct answer on each blank line.

WORD BOX

everything	love
special	campsite
been	tents
hard	idea
what	fire
woods	safe
sounds	

1. *In Act II, Marilyn, Richard, Harry, and Susan arrive at their* _____.

Susan: Oh, I _____ it! I love it!

2. *Harry has _____ camping before, and he knows _____ to do.*

Harry: We'll put _____ over there. We'll set up our _____ over there by the edge of the _____. Then we'll be able to make our _____ there where it's _____.

3. *Later, Marilyn and Richard listen to the _____ of the country.*

Marilyn: I've been having a _____ time keeping my eyes open just listening to it. It's like a _____ music.

4. *And Marilyn gets an _____ . . .*

ACT II

VIDEO GAMES

Scene 1: "You guys are like three kids."

SPLIT DIALOGUE

IN GROUPS OF FOUR

SOUND ON

33:02 - 34:47

Watch the scene. Then work in groups of four. Choose a character and complete that character's dialogue below. Watch the scene as many times as necessary.

SUSAN

1. Oh, I love it! I love it! To be _____ from the city on such a beautiful day is my idea of _____. The grass. The trees. The fresh air.
2. I _____.
3. When you're out in the _____ air like this, it _____ you hungry. Aren't you hungry, Marilyn?

HARRY

1. I _____ you _____ like it. I've _____ doing this for years.
2. Come on, Richard. Help me get this _____ out of the car.
3. Well, we'll put _____ over there. We'll set up our tents over there by the _____ of the woods. Then we'll be able to make our fire there where it's _____.
4. That's _____ makes this spot so _____.
5. We just _____ here.
6. You guys are like three _____.
7. Well, yeah. Now that you _____ it, I guess I am. I mean, how _____ a guy not be hungry with all this _____ about eating?
8. Right here, _____ to the _____ packs. Here. Put the _____ on the picnic table, and I will bring the _____, and the _____ cups.

RICHARD

1. You have the spirit of a _____, Susan. Wait till you see _____ jumping around.
2. Where does it _____?
3. Oh, there's our _____ and _____. All set for eating.
4. _____.
5. _____ you hungry, Harry?

MARILYN

1. That's _____ I love about Susan. She _____ hard. She _____ hard. She's a real Stewart.
2. Is _____ hungry?
3. I _____ am. How _____ you, Richard?
4. Where's the _____ with the chicken _____ sandwiches?

Check your answers with your group.

IN GROUPS OF FIVE

UNDERSTUDIES

Work in groups of five to act out the scene. Four members of the group will play the characters: Susan, Harry, Richard, and Marilyn. One person will be the director. The whole group should study the characters' actions carefully. It is not important to repeat the exact dialogue. Feel free to *improvise*—to change the words, to add new dialogue, or to add new action.

Scene 2: "I've never been more relaxed."

HOW DO RICHARD AND HARRY FEEL?

WITH THE WHOLE CLASS

SOUND ON

34:48 - 35:28

Read the three possible explanations below of Richard's and Harry's feelings. Then watch the scene. Which explanation best describes their feelings? Circle *A*, *B*, or *C*. Explain your choice.

A	B	C
Richard and Harry are happy to have a romantic outing in nature with their wives. Children would ruin the mood.	Richard and Harry are worried about the children, too. They pretend they aren't worried in order to help Marilyn and Susan to relax.	Richard and Harry know the children are safe. Worrying about them will ruin the peace of mind they feel by being out in nature.

Scene 3: "This is heaven, Harry!"

IN OTHER WORDS...

SOUND ON

35:29 - 36:50

Watch the scene. What do the characters mean when they say the underlined parts of the sentences below? Circle *a*, *b*, or *c*.

1. **Susan:** This is heaven, Harry!
   a. an exciting place
   b. a perfect place to be
   c. a place were people go after they die

2. **Harry:** It's refreshing for me.
   a. bringing new energy
   b. a lot of fun
   c. restful

3. **Harry:** I always go back to the city in a wonderful state of mind.
   a. feeling lazy
   b. feeling lost
   c. feeling refreshed and relaxed

4. **Susan:** The office seems so far away.
   a. It was a long trip from my office to here.
   b. My office doesn't seem so important while I'm here.
   c. Now I know I don't really like my job.

Scene 4: "Great idea! Let's do it!"

PAUSE

WITH THE WHOLE CLASS

SOUND ON

36:51 - 38:04

Watch the scene and pause at 37:48. What do you think Marilyn's idea is? Can you guess? Discuss your ideas with the class. Then watch the rest of the scene to find out the answer.

"LET'S GO CAMPING"

WITH THE WHOLE CLASS

SOUND ON

38:05 - 40:03

Watch the "Focus In" segment. Then watch it again and sing along. Here are the words to the song.

Put away your worries.
Put away your cares.
Let's leave our work behind us.
Let's get away somewhere.

Let's pack up what we need,
Enough for a weekend stay.
Let's go on a camping trip,
'Cause we all need to get away.

We'll bring some hot dogs with us,
Burgers and ketchup, too.
Don't forget the mustard,
Because we're going to have
   a barbecue.

We'll pitch our tents right by the
   woods,
And we'll enjoy the view.
The sights and sounds of the
   country
Are waiting for me and you.

**Harry: We'll set up our tents
over there by the edge
of the woods. Then
we'll be able to make
our fire there where
it's safe.**

We'll cook our dinner every night
Over an open fire.
We'll go fishing on the lake,
If we can get a boat for hire.

And if there's any problem—
Something we don't know about—
Park rangers are always there.
They'll always help us out.

We can walk a hiking trail.
There's a lot to see out there.
We can pick some flowers.
You can wear them in your hair.

So pack up your hiking boots,
'Cause you have to dress up right.
And don't forget a lantern,
'Cause it gets real dark at night.

There's always something going on.
There's plenty for us to do.
The sights and sounds of the country
Are waiting for me and you.

INTERMISSION

USEFUL LANGUANGE

In Act II, you heard ways to . . .

• express enthusiasm about
  something:
  I love it!
  This is heaven for me.
• express appreciation of
  someone:
  That's what I like about . . .

• ask for help:
  *Help me get this stuff out of
     the car.*
• ask where to put something:
  Where does it go?
• agree to a suggestion:
  Let's do it.
• say it's too soon after arriving to
  do something:
  We just got here.

• refer to something that
  someone has just said:
  Now that you mention it . . .
• refer to a situation until now:
  How do you like it so far?
• express wishes:
  *I wish we had brought
     Michelle.*
  I wish she were here.
  Wouldn't it be wonderful?

IN PAIRS

INSTANT ROLE-PLAYS

Practice this conversation with a partner:

Getting ready for the camping trip . . .

Camper 1:	Let's check our list. How about hot dogs and hamburgers?
Camper 2:	Hot dogs and hamburgers? Who needs that? We're going to fish and hunt for our food.
Camper 1:	OK. How about the ground cloth and the tent?
Camper 2:	You must be kidding. We don't need tents. We're going to sleep out under the stars.
Camper 1:	How about the cassette player and tapes?
Camper 2:	We're not going to a rock concert. We're going out to enjoy nature.
Camper 1:	And matches.
Camper 2:	Matches?
Camper 1:	I know. You're going to rub two sticks together, right?
Camper 2:	No. We don't need a fire. Remember, when the going gets tough, the tough get going.

Then complete this conversation:

At the campsite that night . . .

Camper 1:	Well, how did the fishing go?
Camper 2:	Not too well.
Camper 1:	
Camper 2:	
Camper 1:	
Camper 2:	
Camper 1:	
Camper 2:	
Camper 1:	
Camper 2:	

ACT III

PREVIEW

SOUND ON

40:09 - 40:36

Watch the preview to complete the sentences below.

1. *In Act III, Richard, Marilyn, Harry, and Susan return home* _____ .

Ellen: Welcome home—and I _____ .

2. *Richard thinks that* _____ .

Richard: _____ ?

3. *And he tries to* _____ .

Richard: _____ .

Ellen: _____ ?

VIDEO GAMES
Scene 1: "What did I tell you?"

SPLIT DIALOGUE

SOUND ON

40:37 - 41:03

Watch the scene. Then work with three other students. Each of you should choose a different character and complete that character's dialogue below. Watch the scene as many times as necessary.

1. MARILYN	2. RICHARD	3. SUSAN	4. HARRY
I'm so glad _____ is _____. I thought Max _____ be _____, and everybody would be _____.	What did I tell you? _____ to _____ about.	I'm sure everything is _____. My mother knows _____ there is to _____ about taking _____ of babies, I _____ you.	Let's put _____ of this _____ away and then take off. We've got a forty-minute _____ into the _____.

Now watch the scene again. Check your answers with your group. Then practice reading the dialogue together.

Scene 2: " . . . and I do mean welcome home."

LISTEN IN

SOUND ON

41:04 - 42:47

Read the statements below. Then watch the scene and listen to it carefully. Which of the following items are true according to the information in the scene? Put a check (✔) in the box only if you are sure the sentence is true.

☐ 1. Max hasn't slept well this weekend.

☐ 2. Ellen is tired from taking care of Max.

☐ 3. Marilyn feels sick, too.

☐ 4. The weather was beautiful for the entire camping trip.

☐ 5. Grandpa took care of Max yesterday afternoon.

☐ 6. Ellen returned late because of the crowds in the village.

☐ 7. Harry used to sell camping equipment.

☐ 8. Marilyn brought some flowers for Ellen.

☐ 9. Harry is going to start a new business.

Scene 3: "It works!"
WHAT'S GOING ON?

SOUND ON
PICTURE OFF

42:48 - 44:41

WITH THE WHOLE CLASS

With the picture off, listen to the scene. (The scene ends when Marilyn says, "The soothing sounds of the country.") Which of the summaries below do you think best describes the action of the scene? Can you guess? Circle A, B, or C. Discuss your ideas with the class. Then turn the picture on and watch the scene to check your answer.

A

Max cries. Richard goes upstairs to play the tape-recorded sounds of the country to Max. Susan and Harry leave. Max stops crying. Richard comes downstairs and plays the sounds for Ellen, and she starts to go to sleep.

B

Max cries. Marilyn and Richard go upstairs to put him to sleep. Susan and Harry leave. Max stops crying. Richard plays the sounds of the country for Ellen and she starts to go to sleep.

C

Max cries. Richard goes upstairs to sing songs to Max. Marilyn goes out with Susan and Harry so they can unpack the car. Richard plays the sounds of the country for Ellen and she goes to sleep.

ACT III

PAST "UNREAL"
WISHES AND CONDITIONS

SOUND ON

44:42 - 46:29

WITH THE WHOLE CLASS

Ellen wishes that Max had felt better. If he had felt better, Ellen would have slept more.

- To express a wish about the past, use the past perfect tense (*had* + past participle) in a *that* clause after the verb *wish*.

  EXAMPLE: Ellen *wishes* that Max *had felt* better.

- To refer to an unreal condition in the past, use the past perfect tense in an *if* clause. Use *would have* + past participle in the main clause.

  EXAMPLE: *If* he *had felt* better, Ellen *would have slept* more.

Watch the "Focus In" segment. Then replay the segment and pause at the three times below. Complete the sentences out loud with the whole class. Repeat the exercise until you can answer without hesitating.

1.
PAUSE AT 45:22

2.
PAUSE AT 45:52

3.
PAUSE AT 46:19

FINALE

READ AND DISCUSS

Read the paragraphs under "U.S. Life." Then discuss your answers to the questions under "Your Turn."

IN SMALL GROUPS

ON YOUR OWN

U.S. LIFE

Richard and Marilyn wouldn't have felt comfortable about going on the camping trip if Ellen hadn't been available to take care of Max. Like many couples in the United States with new babies, their only opportunity to "get away" by themselves for a few days is to have a close relative take care of the child while they are gone.

If close relatives like grandparents or sisters or brothers are unavailable, many couples choose not to take a vacation, or to take their young children with them, rather than have a babysitter take care of the children.

YOUR TURN

1. Do you have children? Do you take them on vacations with you? Why, or why not?
2. How do you feel about leaving babies or young children with a relative for a few days? What about leaving them with a babysitter?

"Opening Night"

In this unit, you will practice . . .

using sounds with meaning
expressing nervousness
talking about what it means to "succeed"

ACT 1

PREVIEW

SOUND ON

48:40 - 49:19

Watch the preview and pause at the three times below. What is the character going to say? Can you guess? Circle *a*, *b*, or *c*.

1.

PAUSE AT 48:47

Carlson:
a. The next thing they'll see is this enlargement with the words "Family Album, U.S.A."
b. The next thing we'll do is have a song entitled, "Family Album, U.S.A."
c. The next thing you'll do is explain the title of your book, "Family Album, U.S.A."

2.

PAUSE AT 48:58

Richard:
a. I'm completely calm.
b. I'm scared to death.
c. I'm feeling sick.

3.

PAUSE AT 49:09

Carlson:
a. Mitchell is one of the best photographers in the country.
b. Mitchell is one of the most important syndicated reviewers in the country.
c. Mitchell is one of my best friends in the country.

VIDEO GAMES

Scene 1: "... a dream come true."

LISTEN IN

SOUND ON

49:20 - 54:23

Read the statements below. Then watch all of Act I and listen to it carefully. Which of the following items are true according to the information in the scene? Put a check (✔) in the box only if you are sure the sentence is true.

☐ **1.** People are going to write about Richard's photos in the newspaper.

☐ **2.** Richard's next book is going to be about houses.

☐ **3.** Carlson wants Richard to sign copies of the book for people who attend the exhibit.

☐ **4.** Everyone who comes to the exhibit will get a free book.

☐ **5.** Richard's family will stay close to him during the exhibit.

☐ **6.** Mitchell Johnson writes reviews for papers all over the United States.

☐ **7.** Mitchell usually tries to help good young photographers.

☐ **8.** Carlson is not sure whether Mitchell likes Richard's photographs or not.

☐ **9.** Tom has never published a book of his own photographs.

☐ **10.** Mitchell thinks that Richard has a unique way of seeing things.

☐ **11.** Mitchell does not say whether he likes Richard's photographs or not.

☐ **12.** Mitchell's review will appear in the evening paper today.

IN SMALL GROUPS

CRITICS' CHOICE

SOUND ON

52:12 - 53:02

A. Watch this part of the scene again. Then match the photo descriptions and categories below. Choose the category that best applies to the photo. Write the letter of the correct category on the blank line beside each photo description. The same category may be used more than once.

_____ **1.** t-shirt vendor
_____ **2.** Central Park carriage
_____ **3.** street crowd
_____ **4.** basketball game
_____ **5.** New York skyline
_____ **6.** traffic policeman
_____ **7.** roller coaster ride
_____ **8.** exercise class

a. human interest
b. organized sports
c. fun and excitement
d. panoramic views
e. on the job
f. keeping fit
g. city scenes

B. Which photo do you like best? Why? Discuss your choice with your group.

IN OTHER WORDS...

SOUND ON

49:20 - 54:23

Watch all of Act I again. Then read the sentences below. What do each of the <u>underlined</u> parts of the sentences mean? Circle *a*, *b*, or *c*.

1. "It <u>sets the tone for</u> the whole show."
   a. looks like everything in
   b. prepares people for the feeling of
   c. suggests music for

2. "...it's still <u>a dream come true</u>."
   a. something I saw in my sleep
   b. something I hoped wouldn't happen
   c. something I hoped would happen

3. "I hope he's <u>in a good mood</u>."
   a. feeling happy
   b. feeling serious
   c. a good writer

4. "It's <u>common practice</u>."
   a. something usually done
   b. the least one can do
   c. not necessary

5. "I'm <u>scared to death</u>."
   a. afraid I might die
   b. a little nervous
   c. very afraid

6. "They've <u>stood by me</u> through all this."
   a. given me money
   b. given me encouragement
   c. helped me take the photos

7. "...mind if I look around and see <u>what it says to me</u>?"
   a. what you wanted to express
   b. how I feel about it
   c. why you published it

8. "You may be <u>the next Ansel Adams</u>..."
   a. as well known as Ansel Adams
   b. better than Ansel Adams
   c. almost as good as Ansel Adams

9. "You have <u>a most unusual eye</u>."
   a. a complicated way of seeing life
   b. a funny way of seeing life
   c. a unique way of seeing life

10. "<u>Keep your fingers crossed</u>."
    a. Hope for the best.
    b. Don't worry about it.
    c. Think positively.

SOUNDS WITH MEANING

IN PAIRS

SOUND ON

54:24 - 55:47

A. Watch the "Focus In" segment. Then, with a partner, take turns reading the statements below. Your partner should respond with an appropriate sound from the Sound Box. Some of the sounds can be used more than once. If you are not sure of the meaning of some of the sounds, look at the Useful Language box on the next page.

1. Do you understand this exercise?
2. Guess what? I found out who borrowed your book. It was Albert!
3. For lunch, we're having peanut butter and banana sandwiches.
4. How did you like the meeting on new theories of grammar?
5. Want to see a movie tonight?
6. How about seeing "The Loves of an International Spy"?
7. Guess what? You won the lottery for $1 million!
8. Just kidding.
9. If you won a million dollars, would you spend half and save half, or save half and spend half?
10. Seriously, if you won a million dollars, how much would you save, how much would you donate to charities, how much would you spend, and what would you buy?

SOUND BOX

Hmm.

Uh-uh.

Uh-huh.

Huh?

Ah-hah!

Yuk!

Ho-hum.

Ooh!

Aww.

WITH THE WHOLE CLASS

B. Take turns answering each part of the last question in Activity A. Then the whole class should respond to each answer with appropriate sounds from the Sound Box.

ACT I

INTERMISSION

USEFUL LANGUAGE

In Act I, you heard ways to . . .

- express astonishment:
  I can't believe this is really happening.
  It's a dream come true.

- express uncertainty:
  You never know . . .

- say you feel happy:
  I'm in a good mood.

- say something goes against your value system:
  I feel uncomfortable about it.

- express anxiety:
  I'm scared to death.

- ask the significance of something:
  What does [that] mean . . .?

- use sounds to express meaning:
  I'm thinking: *Hmm.*
  No.: *Uh-uh.*
  Yes.: *Uh-huh.*
  What?: *Huh?*
  I understand.: *Ah-hah!*
  Terrible!: *Yuk!*
  Boring.: *Ho-hum.*
  Exciting!: *Ooh!*
  Too bad.: *Aww.*

IN PAIRS

INSTANT ROLE-PLAYS

Practice this conversation with a partner:

At the last class of the semester . . .

Teacher:	Shall we have a test today?
Students:	Uh-uh.
Teacher:	OK. How about looking at some slides of my stamp collection?
Students:	Ho-hum.
Teacher:	How about a class party?
Students:	Uh-huh!
Teacher:	OK. Everybody will perform a song or dance for the class.
Students:	Ooh!
Teacher:	But first we'll have a little end-of-semester quiz.
Students:	Aww.

Then complete this conversation:

Planning for the class reunion . . .

A: OK, what shall we do for this year's class reunion?
B:
A:
B:

A:
B:
A:
B:

A:

B:

READ AND DISCUSS

Read the paragraphs under "U.S. Life." Then discuss your answers to the questions under "Your Turn."

ON YOUR OWN

U.S. LIFE

An exhibition at a private art gallery is a way of introducing a new artist to the public. The idea is to stage an event that will create interest in the artist and stimulate sales of his or her work.

Exhibitions of painting, sculpture, and photography at public museums and galleries are different from private showings. The works exhibited at public museums are by established, well-known artists. Many exhibitions include works from the museum's **permanent collection**—that is, works owned by the museum.

Public museums and galleries also exhibit works by a particular artist, or works from a particular period, that are not part of their own permanent collection. They borrow the works from the permanent collections of other museums. Admission is charged to cover the cost of the event. The works are not offered for sale.

IN SMALL GROUPS

YOUR TURN

1. Do you have a favorite artist or photographer? What do you like about his or her work?

2. Have you ever had an exhibition of something you made? If so, tell the class about it.

3. What is the most interesting exhibition you have ever attended?

PREVIEW

SOUND OFF

55:53 - 56:25

Read the three dialogues below. Then, with the sound off, watch the preview. Which dialogue is correct for the preview? Can you guess? Circle A, B, or C.

	A
Marilyn:	What are you looking for?
Richard:	I lost my stupid cuff link. I'll look like a fool at the showing with one sleeve undone.

	B
Marilyn:	What are you waiting for?
Richard:	Forget the whole thing. I can't go through with it. I'm just too nervous.

	C
Marilyn:	What are you afraid of?
Richard:	Everything. A critic was there this morning. He probably hates my work.

Now, with the sound on, watch the preview again to check your answer.

ACT II

VIDEO GAMES

Scene 1: "As soon as I recover from my nervous breakdown."

THE SUBTEXT

SOUND ON

56:26 - 58:45

Read Marilyn's and Richard's thoughts below. Then watch the scene again and listen to the conversation carefully. What do the characters say to express these thoughts? Tell your teacher to stop the tape when you hear each answer. Repeat the character's actual dialogue.

1

Marilyn: **Think positively and you will be fine.**

3

Richard: **I'm not sure I'm good enough for this.**

2

Marilyn: *I love you, too.*

4

Richard: *I want to be an artist, not a promoter.*

Scene 2: "Charmed."

SCRIPTWRITERS

SOUND OFF

58:46 - 1:00:23

With the sound off, watch the scene. Then do the activities below.

A. In what sequence did the pictured events occur? To show the correct order, write a number from *1* to *3* in the box at the top right of each picture.

B. What do you think the characters are saying? Write dialogue for the characters on the blank lines beside each picture.

a. Richard: _____

_____

Carlson: _____

Marilyn: _____

b. Philip: _____

_____

Carlson: _____

_____

c. Carlson: _____

_____

Grandpa: _____

_____

C. Now, <u>with the sound on</u>, watch the scene. Which do you prefer—the dialogue you wrote above, or the dialogue in the scene?

IN SMALL GROUPS

MYSTERY GUEST

A. Work in small groups. Choose a host for each group. Your teacher will introduce the whole class to a Mystery Guest. The host of each group will introduce the members of his or her group to the Mystery Guest. To prepare for the introductions, follow the instructions in the boxes below.

HOSTS

Think of one or two things you have learned about each member of your group during this course. The group members will help you. You will include these facts about each group member when you introduce him or her to the Mystery Guest. Write the facts on the blank lines below.

Name: _____

Fact #1: _____

Fact #2: _____

Name: _____

Fact #1: _____

Fact #2: _____

Name: _____

Fact #1: _____

Fact #2: _____

Name: _____

Fact #1: _____

Fact #2: _____

GROUP MEMBERS

Help your host think of one or two facts about you. For example:

1. What is your native country?
2. How long have you been studying English?
3. What do you hope to do with your knowledge of English?
4. What work do you do, or hope to do?

The host will include these facts when he or she introduces you to the Mystery Guest.

B. Now you are ready to meet the Mystery Guest! Each host should introduce the group members to the Mystery Guest. Then take turns asking questions to find out as much as possible about the Mystery Guest.

"I'M NERVOUS"

SOUND ON

1:00:24 - 1:02:02

Watch the "Focus In" segment. Then watch it again and sing along. Here are the words to the song.

Carlson: Nervous about the opening tonight?
Richard: Nervous? Me? No. I'm scared to death.

I'm nervous.
I'm scared to death.
My heart is pounding like a drum,
And I'm out of breath.

Ooh, I'm nervous!
I can't think straight.
My palms are sweaty, I can't relax,
And I just can't concentrate.

I've got butterflies in my stomach.
And look at my hands!
         They shake!
I try to get to sleep at night.
         But I lie there wide awake . . .
'Cause I'm nervous!
Oh, I'm just a mess. Yeah!
My mouth is dry,
I can hardly speak,
And I can't even get myself dressed.

Richard: I earned this, and I'm going to enjoy it.
         As soon as I recover from my nervous
         breakdown.

Ooh, I'm nervous!
It's my opening night.
I'm weak in the knees, I'm fidgety,
And I'm beside myself with fright.

I've got butterflies in my stomach.
And look at my hands!
         They shake!
I try to get to sleep at night.
         But I lie there wide awake . . .
'Cause I'm nervous!

And it's easy to see.
I'm jumpy. I'm jittery.
I'm anxious and panicky.
Ooh, I'm nervous!
Yeah, I'm nervous!

I'm scared to death.

ACT II

INTERMISSION

USEFUL LANGUAGE

In Act II, you heard the following ways to express nervousness . . .

I'm nervous.
I'm scared to death.
My heart is pounding like a drum
I'm out of breath.
I can't think straight.
My palms are sweaty.
I can't relax.
I just can't concentrate.

I've got butterflies in my stomach.
My hands shake.
I try to get to sleep at night, but I
lie there wide awake.
I'm just a mess.
My mouth is dry.
I can hardly speak.

I'm weak in the knees.
I'm fidgety.
I'm beside myself with fright.
I'm jumpy.
I'm jittery.
I'm anxious.
I'm panicky.

↕

INSTANT ROLE-PLAYS

IN PAIRS

Practice this conversation with a partner:

Before the championship football game . . .

Star player: What's the matter, coach? You look tired.
Coach: I tried to sleep last night but I lay there awake, thinking about this game.
Star player: We're ready for this game, coach.
Coach: But have you seen the size of the other team's players?
Star player: They're pretty big, coach, but we can handle them.
Coach: I feel weak in the knees. I hope they don't hurt you guys too badly.
Star player: Just relax and enjoy the game, coach.
Coach: Do you think we should call it off? I mean, you guys could get killed.
Star player: Coach, we earned the right to be in this game and we're going through with it.
Coach: I want to write out some plays for you, but my hands are shaking too badly.
Star player: Just tell them to us.
Coach: No good. My mouth is too dry. I can't speak. Uh-oh. It's time to go out and play.
Star player: Coach, before we go onto the field, I just want to tell you that you've always been an inspiration to us.

Then complete this conversation:

After the game . . .

Sports reporter: Well, coach, your team played a great game. How did you do it?

Coach:
Sports reporter:

Coach:

Sports reporter:

Coach:
Sports reporter:

Coach:

Sports reporter:

Coach:
Sports reporter:

Coach:

ON YOUR OWN

STORYWRITER

By yourself, write about one of the following:

• **Write a short sports story about a football game based on the interview you just role-played.**
• **Write about the event in your life that made you the most nervous.**
• **Write the whole story of Act II.**

PREVIEW

Read the three summaries below. Then, with the sound off, watch the preview. Which summary best describes the preview? Can you guess? Circle A, B, or C.

SOUND OFF

1:02:08 - 1:02:55

A

The review of Richard's work is not favorable. But an art critic, Mr. O'Neill, wants Richard to work for his newspaper as a writer.

B

The review of Richard's work is in the newspaper. A magazine publisher, Mr. O'Neill, wants Richard to work for him.

C

The review of Richard's work is favorable. A camera manufacturer, Mr. O'Neill, offers Richard a job testing new photo equipment.

Now, with the sound on, watch the preview to check your answer.

VIDEO GAMES

Scene 1: "Wow! I'm overwhelmed."

SPLIT DIALOGUE

IN GROUPS OF THREE

SOUND ON

1:02:56 - 1:04:47

Watch the scene. Then work with two other students. One of you will complete Richard's lines; one will complete Harvey Carlson's; the third student will complete Marilyn's. Watch the scene as many times as necessary.

RICHARD

1. What's _____?
2. I _____. Would you read _____, Marilyn?
3. Wow! I'm _____.
4. Hello. I want to thank all of you for _____ here tonight. I'd like to thank Harvey Carlson for his _____ in my project. But _____ of all, I would like to thank my family for their love and _____ all through this _____. Thank you.

HARVEY CARLSON

1. _____ it.
2. _____!
3. Ladies and gentlemen, if I may have your _____ for a _____, please? I hope you're all _____ the exhibition. I know that I _____. And I would like to _____ the young man who spent the last _____ years taking these _____ pictures and writing the _____ for *Family Album, U.S.A.*—Mr. Richard Stewart.

MARILYN

1. "Richard Stewart's _____ at the Carlson Gallery is a _____ of photographs from his new book _____ *Family Album, U.S.A.* There is _____ and _____ in Mr. Stewart's work, and his book introduces us to a _____ new _____." Oh, Richard, it's _____!

Now watch the scene again. Check your answers with your group. Then practice reading the dialogue together.

Scene 2: *"Oh, I'm glad that's over."*
TAKE A GUESS

IN PAIRS

SOUND OFF

1:04:48 - 1:07:21

Read the questions below. Then, with the sound off, watch the scene. Work with a partner to guess the answers to the questions. Then, with the sound on, watch the scene to check your answers.

1. Why does the photographer want pictures of Richard and Marilyn?
2. What type of job does O'Neill offer Richard?
3. Does Richard accept the job?
4. Is Marilyn pleased or disappointed with Richard's decision?

IN OTHER WORDS . . .

Watch the scene again. What do the underlined words and phrases mean? Circle *a*, *b*, or *c*.

1. "I'll <u>settle for</u> an 'A' in my photography course."
   a. probably get
   b. be happy with
   c. be lucky to get
2. "I'm really <u>impressed by your show</u>."
   a. I'm really happy that your show is a success.
   b. I'm amazed at how good your show is.
   c. I'm surprised that so many people were at your show.
3. ". . . <u>where would I fit into the plan?</u>"
   a. what would my role be?
   b. who will my boss be?
   c. whose idea is it?
4. "I'd like you to be <u>the photo editor</u> of the magazine."
   a. the person who chooses which photos to use
   b. the person who takes the photos
   c. the person who gives classes to the photographers
5. "I'm <u>flattered</u>, but I enjoy taking pictures . . ."
   a. feeling embarrassed
   b. feeling pleased
   c. feeling complimented

OUR FAMILY ALBUM

SOUND ON

1:07:22 - 1:10:19

Watch the "Focus In" segment. Then watch it again and pick five photographs that you'd like to write about. Choose pictures of the members of the Stewart family that you like best, or of scenes that you remember best. For each photograph that you choose, answer the questions below.

1. *Who* are the characters in the picture?
2. *What* was happening in the scene?
3. *Where* did the scene take place?

FINALE

READ AND DISCUSS

Read the paragraphs under "U.S. Life." Then discuss your answers to the questions under "Your Turn."

ON YOUR OWN

U.S. LIFE

One of the enduring myths about the United States is that of the "overnight success"—the person who wakes up to discover that he or she is suddenly wealthy and famous. Although this may happen occasionally, it does not represent how people succeed in the United States. In Richard's case, he achieved recognition after five years of hard work. Even so, it usually takes more than a single exhibition, or a single favorable newspaper review, to attain success. Furthermore, the kind of "instant" success that Richard won is not typical.

The United States is made up of men and women who spend their working lives in responsible and productive jobs outside the spotlight of public recognition, for modest financial rewards. In fact, most Americans do not measure success in terms of fame or great wealth. For them, being a success means having a sense of self-worth —feeling good about themselves and what they do.

IN SMALL GROUPS

YOUR TURN

1. Are you successful? What does "success" mean to you? Is it the same as your worth as an individual?
2. Are success and self-worth measured differently in your country than they are in the United States? Explain.